W9-AXD-577

A Totally Difficult Decision

Suddenly, everyone was staring at me. Usually that is so not a problem. But, I have to admit, I was just a smidge unsure of myself.

If I *was* going to enter the writing contest, it wasn't going to be because of Amber.

I glanced at the book lying between Brandon and me. There on the jacket was Troy, the well-toned, blemish-free, most-wanted cover boy in America.

"So, girlfriend," De prodded, all psyched, "are you going to write the book of love and snag that dream date with Troy?"

I looked up, and my eyes met Brandon's. The dark-haired young poet, who reminded me of like Ethan Hawke and Matt Damon and Ben Affleck and all the adorable wannabe award-winning writers in L.A., was smiling at me. He was waiting for my answer, too.

"I don't know," I confessed. "It's like a major maybe."

Clueless® Books

CLUELESS™ • A novel by H. B. Gilmour
  Based on the film written and directed by Amy Heckerling
CHER'S GUIDE TO . . . WHATEVER • H. B. Gilmour
CHER NEGOTIATES NEW YORK • Jennifer Baker
AN AMERICAN BETTY IN PARIS • Randi Reisfeld
ACHIEVING PERSONAL PERFECTION • H. B. Gilmour
CHER'S FURIOUSLY FIT WORKOUT • Randi Reisfeld
FRIEND OR FAUX • H. B. Gilmour
CHER GOES ENVIRO-MENTAL • Randi Reisfeld
BALDWIN FROM ANOTHER PLANET • H. B. Gilmour
TOO HOTTIE TO HANDLE • Randi Reisfeld
CHER AND CHER ALIKE • H. B. Gilmour
TRUE BLUE HAWAII • Randi Reisfeld
ROMANTICALLY CORRECT • H. B. Gilmour
A TOTALLY CHER AFFAIR • H. B. Gilmour
CHRONICALLY CRUSHED • Randi Reisfeld
BABES IN BOYLAND • H. B. Gilmour
DUDE WITH A 'TUDE • Randi Reisfeld
CHER'S FRANTICALLY ROMANTIC ASSIGNMENT
  • H. B. Gilmour

Available from ARCHWAY Paperbacks

For orders other than by individual consumers, Pocket Books
grants a discount on the purchase of **10 or more** copies of
single titles for special markets or premium use. For further
details, please write to the Vice-President of Special Markets,
Pocket Books, 1633 Broadway, New York, NY 10019-6785,
8th Floor.

For information on how individual consumers can place
orders, please write to Mail Order Department, Simon &
Schuster Inc., 200 Old Tappan Road, Old Tappan, NJ 07675.

Cher's
Frantically
Romantic
Assignment

H.B. Gilmour

AN ARCHWAY PAPERBACK
Published by POCKET BOOKS
New York London Toronto Sydney Tokyo Singapore

The sale of this book without its cover is unauthorized. If you purchased
this book without a cover, you should be aware that it was reported to
the publisher as "unsold and destroyed." Neither the author nor the
publisher has received payment for the sale of this "stripped book."

This book is a work of fiction. Names, characters, places and
incidents are products of the author's imagination or are used
fictitiously. Any resemblance to actual events or locales or persons,
living or dead, is entirely coincidental.

AN ARCHWAY PAPERBACK *Original*

An Archway Paperback published by
POCKET BOOKS, a division of Simon & Schuster Inc.
1230 Avenue of the Americas, New York, NY 10020

™, ® and Copyright © 1998 by Paramount Pictures

All rights reserved, including the right to reproduce
this book or portions thereof in any form whatsoever.
For information address Pocket Books, 1230 Avenue
of the Americas, New York, NY 10020

ISBN: 0-671-02091-9

First Archway Paperback printing December 1998

10 9 8 7 6 5 4 3 2 1

AN ARCHWAY PAPERBACK and colophon are
registered trademarks of Simon & Schuster Inc.

Printed in the U.S.A.

IL: 7+

For Anne, New York's #1 *Clueless* fan,
and her peerless pal, Rodger.
With thanks to Dorothy Dubrule,
for her enthusiasm and assistance.
And to Jessi, as always, with love.

Cher's Frantically Romantic Assignment

Chapter 1

*H*el-*lo,* is this the Beverly Center or the San Diego Zoo?" my best friend, Dionne, asked, pushing through a crowd of ballistic bargain hunters who were storming the Gap.

Suddenly a random raver in elephant pants and platform sneakers crashed into the shopping bags I was carrying.

"That reckless stooge just scuffed my Birkenstocks," our friend Summer wailed, staring down at her trashed sandals.

"Saturday at the mall can so reek," I agreed.

Big surprise.

I mean, it was the weekend after a holiday. Which is when every disappointed dork in the greater Los Angeles shopping area shows up all desperate to return the lame sweater his mom bought him and cash in his Record-Town gift certificate.

But we had no choice.

De and I were at the mall on a rescue mission. We had promised to help Summer find a choice outfit for this romantic fiesta her family was throwing.

After being together longer than Hootie and the Blowfish, Summer's mom and dad had decided to pledge their love anew in this fabulous, fully catered anniversary bash.

Summer, who is a serious animal rights activist and part-time vegetarian, was frantic for a decent outfit to wear to the gala.

She was all, "Oh, Cher, I saw this brutally jiggy silk chemise trimmed in synthetic fur. So I thought that was okay. I mean, the fur was faux, right? But then I caught a Discovery Channel segment on silkworms, and I went like 'Gross. Is that where they get silk from? Worms?' And now I'm frenzied. I don't have anything to wear. Cher, I need your help."

Which she so did. And which De and I would definitely have donated even if she hadn't asked.

Dionne and I are black belt shoppers, big time. We're also chronic at makeovers. In addition to being furiously popular Bettys—bright, attractive, and allowancely abled—we are mega-gifted in ensemble selection. Next to filling our own walk-in closets with color-coordinated rows of scrumptious designer originals, De and I love dressing up our peers.

For today's do-good junket, my true blue was wearing a def mint tank top and matching drawstring pants with relaxed boot-leg styling. She had loosely braided her rich dark hair and topped it off with a Dolce & Gabbana silk bandana.

With her tawny complexion and exotic hazel eyes, the

braids 'n' bandana thing so worked for De. On me, it would have been way too Pippi Longstocking.

All shimmering blond hair and blue eyes, I'd left my lustrous pH-balanced locks loose and long. Which looked furiously fresh with the baby-blue cropped V-neck cardigan and double side-striped nylon mesh pants I was sporting.

In contrast, Summer was all in environmentally correct itchy natural fibers, accessorized with seashell earrings and a henna hand tattoo.

"This place is so the mental mosh pit," she declared, adjusting her Friends of the Earth pin. "I'm way sorry I dragged you guys here."

"Don't go there," I said, holding up a hand moisturized with rich emollients and firming kelp. "It isn't every day a girl's parents celebrate their love for each other."

"In front of five hundred people," Summer reported.

"Whew, where are they throwing it?" I said. "At Dodger Stadium?"

"That would be too cramped," Summer said. "At home."

"At my parents' recommitment ceremony there were five hundred *tables* of people," De reminisced as we stepped onto the up escalator. "And each table had these heart-shaped little candle glasses, which we thought the guests would take home. Not. Our garage is still stacked to the ceiling with them."

"Anyway, Summer, De and I were glad to help you choose a props frock for the gala," I assured our bud.

"That slinky red chemise we found at Bloomie's turned you into a serious Shalom," De said as we soared toward the Beverly Center's eighth and final floor. "Now all we have to do is pick out a def present for Goldie and Chuck and this mall is so history."

De and I had been invited to the upcoming romantic blowout. Which meant we had to find a suitable gift for the occasion. Since Summer's parents, Goldie and Chuck Finkel-Dworkin, lived in Beverly Hills, the total consumer capital of the world, finding them a trinket they didn't already own was a mighty challenge.

"We can do this," I reminded my crew, as we stepped off the escalator. "I mean, we're here at L.A.'s foremost center for fashion, food, and film."

"Lured by a selection of more than one hundred and sixty upscale boutiques, restaurants, and entertainment complexes," De added. "There's gotta be something dope in seven acres of shopping ops that your parents would like."

The sight of a frenzied mob gathered before the bookstore inspired me. "How about a keepsake wedding album?" I suggested. "You know, like a book where they can fill in dates and details, and guests can sign it and wish them well and all?"

"Excellent!" Summer exclaimed as we moved toward the unruly crowd.

The gathering seemed way rowdy for fans of reading. Hordes of frantic females milled outside the bookstore, blocking the entrance. Many of them, I noticed as we scooched through the herd, were clutching the same colorful paperback.

"Excuse me, what book is that?" I asked this flipped-out girl in our path.

"It's only like *What the Heart Remembers,*" she shouted above the shrieking mob. "Ani K. Niel's romantic new blockbuster." She flashed the book jacket at me.

On the cover this fiercely props, pectorally abled guy

was sweeping a swooning Yasmine Bleeth–type heroine off her feet. His long golden hair, excellently highlighted with platinum streaks, framed the chiseled face of a monsterly buff babe.

I plucked the book from the girl's hands. "De, look. Isn't that Troy?" I asked, studying the studly cover boy.

De leaned over to gaze at the chronic hunk. "Hel-*lo,* he's only the most famous book model of our day," she affirmed.

"Did you catch him on Sally Jessy's 'Gorgeous Guys Who Drive Women Wild' segment?" Summer asked. "Troy was the hands-down Adonis of the entire beefy bunch."

"Well, he's here," enthused the fan, snatching back her book. "And I'm going to get his autograph."

"Troy is here?" De craned her slender neck, trying to catch a glimpse of the muscular muffin above the crowd of boisterous book lovers. *"The* Troy?"

"Well, duh." Another Betty clutching a copy of *What the Heart Remembers* spun to face us. "Like who do you think we're screaming for, Charles Dickens?"

"Ooo, I'd love to see Troy up close," Summer squealed. "Even if he did wear fur on the cover of *Wild Fury.* I mean, it was just a loincloth and probably faux."

"Excuse me. We have a present to purchase," I reminded my buds, leading them through the wriggling wall of fans. We pushed slowly toward the bookstore entrance.

Suddenly, I came to a standstill. I found myself pressed against this chain that marked the beginning of the autographing area. Like ecstatic toddlers on their way to meet Santa, a long line of book-toting fans was shuffling through the roped-off maze.

"Where's your book?" A large woman in a heinously generic skirt and sweater set was suddenly in my face.

"I don't have one," I said. "My friends and I are just trying to get inside to buy a gift." I looked over my shoulder and saw that De and Summer were caught in a jam. They were stuck several fans back.

Suddenly this commanding voice rang out. "It's okay, Corky. Let her through." And about a million girls started screeching.

Obediently, Corky, the plus-size gatekeeper, stepped aside.

Behind her, at the end of the winding, roped-off path, bathed in the warm glow of a soft spotlight that lit the silver streaks in his long, golden hair, stood this bitterly outstanding hottie.

His emerald green eyes flashed as they met my clear, cornflower blue gaze. I felt the urge to look away, but I couldn't even blink. And not because I was afraid my new Le Grand Curl lift-and-lengthen L'Oréal mascara would crack and shed unsightly freckles across my suddenly warm, porcelain cheeks.

Seeming not to notice the girls tearing at his Ultra-suede vest, Troy walked toward me.

The piercing adolescent shrieks around us faded to a dull roar. The hyper crowd blurred into one multicolored Benetton smudge. Everything seemed to move in slow motion. Except my thundering heart.

"Who are you?" the ripply muscled hunk asked.

"Cher Horowitz," I replied. "I love those buckskin breeches. Are they like Prada?"

"Leather Loft," he said, reaching out gently to touch my hair. "Did Chris at Estillo do your highlights?"

"No, it was Ivan, the colorist at Rocket," I told him. "He's totally epic."

The fierce Fabio laughed, revealing these dazzling ultrabright teeth. "Is it hard to get an appointment with him?"

"Use my name," I suggested. "We have this excellent relationship. Here." I dug into my petite Escada purse and pulled out one of the adorable business cards Daddy had made up for me. They're creamy off-white with my name, number, and E-mail address embossed in this classic pink script.

"Troy," Corky interrupted us. "There are about a hundred people lined up. Give the kid an autograph and let's move it along."

"I don't have a book," I said.

"Buy one," Corky grumbled.

Troy gave her this look.

"Here." Corky thrust a copy of Ani K. Niel's romance novel into his hands, and he scribbled a message inside, then gave me the book. "Nice meeting you, Cher," he said, tucking my card into his vest and touching my hair once more. "Ivan knows what he's doing."

As Troy started back to his autographing table, De and Summer made their way toward me through the crowd.

"Cher, I'm like busting with pride, totally kvelling," De announced, squeezing between two girls waiting on line for their encounter with Attila the Hunk.

"I saw him sign your book. What did he write?" Summer clamored.

"I don't know. I haven't looked at it yet," I confessed. Before I could peer at the inscription, De pressed her palm to my forehead.

"Girlfriend," my concerned bud said, "you look all flushed and Kevin Spacey. Are you okay?"

"Actually," I had to admit, "I feel kind of weird. When I got to the autographing area where Troy was signing books, everything went all blurry. Voices faded. I could barely focus on anything."

"Sounds like love," Summer crooned.

"Sounds like low blood sugar," De decided, checking her neon faced TAG Heuer watch. "It's way past lunch time, and I bet you skipped breakfast, even though it's the most important meal of the day."

"How did you know?" I asked, realizing that it was true. I was woozy with hunger.

"Easy. 'Cause like I did, too," De replied, taking my arm and shoving and schlepping us back through the mob. "Somewhere between floss and shower, shampoo and moisturize, my Eat Now command got carelessly deleted."

"I'm totally starving," I said. "Let's refuel."

It took us a moment to settle on a venue. Weak with hunger and mall overload, I was all, "Okay, Hard Rock or Todai?" But De thought CPK or Gaucho Grill.

"Where do you want to eat?" We turned to Summer for the deciding vote.

"I can't go," she announced, running a henna-decorated hand through her healthy, herbally conditioned hair. "I've got an aromatherapy session scheduled in like fifteen minutes. Then I've got to rehearse the speech I'm supposed to give at my parents' bash. Plus I'm like still stuffed from brunch. Froma, our Israeli housekeeper, force fed me lox, eggs, and onions this morning."

"Yuck, yolks and all?" I asked, aghast. "Eggs are such a cholesterol fest."

"Not even. It was egg whites only," Summer explained. "Thanks for all your help today. You guys are so the bomb. Catch you later."

We exchanged air kisses and limp-wristed Beverly Hills high fives. Then Summer split.

"It doesn't really matter where we gorge. We're just getting mixed greens and Evian anyway," De reminded me. "Let's go generic. The food court's around the corner."

My bud was correct, I knew. Not so much about our dining options as about the fact that my lightheadedness was more about hunger than hunks.

Still, my brief encounter with the blond hottie haunted me. As I followed my best through the stooge-rich rabble of Saturday shoppers, I couldn't help wondering: Would I ever run into the buff cover boy again?

Chapter 2

*T*he binge barn was brutally packed. We hit the salad bar, loaded up our trays, then scanned the tumultuous space for a place to sit down.

Looking needy yet chronic, De and I waited at the edge of the crowded dining area.

It took about three seconds.

This table full of boys blowing spitballs at each other through Orange Julius straws noticed us.

They froze midblast. Their eyes swept over us, taking in the excellent cut of our pastel casuals, our firm, slender arms laden with trays and shopping bags, and our classic faces framed by different yet equally heart-stopping hairsdos.

De blinked her double set of dark lashes at them.

I smiled with my perfect, pinkly glossed lips.

The trio at the table scrambled to their Nike-clad feet,

waving us over, and going, "Sit here. Choose us. Take this table! We're leaving. This seat's available!"

They cleared their paper cups, straws, and spitballs, and gallantly made way for us.

"This is so clean of you," I thanked them.

"Nothing's too good for you, Cher," the tallest of the spitball blowers vowed. He tossed his head, knocking back a wing of glossy dark hair that had flopped down over one eye.

"You know me?" I asked.

"Oh, no," his friend interrupted. "Like we really skipped Cher-and-De class, and now we gotta take a makeup test on who the most popular Bettys of Bronson Alcott High School are. Duh, Brandon, help me here."

"Brandon?" De snapped her manicured fingers. "You're in Mr. Stanky's English class with us, aren't you?" she asked the dark-haired one, who had the cutest little slacker soul patch in the hollow between his lip and chin.

It gave his grinning face this Ethan Hawke-ish sensitivity that I'd never noticed before. Actually, I'd never really noticed the boy, let alone his midchin facial hairs.

He shrugged now. "I'm the one," he said. "See you on Monday."

"You know that guy?" I asked De as we unloaded our trays and sat down.

"Not really," she confessed. "I mean, when his Moe friend mentioned his name, I had this mini-blip of recognition. I think he sits behind Amber in English. Which makes it hard yet not impossible for her to cheat off him." De plucked a wilted lettuce leaf from her plastic bowl and examined it. "Yuck, iceberg," she complained.

"Gee, Toto," I teased her, "I guess we're not in Spago anymore."

"We should have carbo-loaded curly fries," my bud observed.

Suddenly Summer ran up to our table. She was carrying a little paper bag and a food container that looked like the ones Sam Chen's China Bowl on Wilshire packed rice in for deliveries. She wasn't holding the carton by its thin metal handle, she was cradling it against her scratchy shirt.

"Did you cancel your aromatherapy and pick up some dim sum?" I asked.

"No," Summer said, all grinning and aglow. "I got you guys a thank-you gift for helping me today."

"You got us Chinese food?" De asked.

"No way," Summer protested, setting down the paper bag and the container. "There was only one left. Okay, well. Thanks for everything. I've gotta run."

"You shouldn't have," I called after her as De checked out our gift.

"Summer, get back here!" De shouted suddenly.

"What is it?" I asked, peering into the carton my bud had opened.

"A fish!" De replied. We both stared into the cramped paper box and watched this really sweet little iridescent goldfish swimming in tight circles. He was fully attractive, all graceful and plump.

"What's in the bag?" I wondered aloud.

"Knowing Summer," De said, "it's probably some endangered insect or rodent."

Cautiously, we opened the paper bag. "It's fish food and care and feeding instructions," I announced, relieved.

"Okay," De said. "I'll take the instructions, you take the fish."

"He is kind of cute, don't you think?" I ventured.

"I can see you've already bonded. That's great," De said. "I don't have much luck with fish. The few I've had went belly up faster than the Spice Girls. Why don't you take it?"

"We can take turns, do joint custody," I suggested. "I'll keep him this week, okay?"

"Cher, you're looking at heartbreak with fins," De said gravely. "Forget feeding instructions, they should come with a CPR manual. Good luck, girlfriend."

While I closed the little carton and carefully tucked it into my Escada tote, De glanced over at my book.

"What the Heart Remembers by Ani K. Niel. I think my mom reads her stuff. She's written like a gazillion bestsellers. So what did the cover hottie write inside?" she asked, opening the book.

"Oooo, here it is. Eew, he drew a smiley face."

"Not even," I said in disbelief.

"He did," De insisted. Then she grinned. "Right under this part—where he says he's going to *call you!*"

"Not even, squared!" I exclaimed. Grabbing back the book, I read the inscription aloud: " 'For Cher. I'll call soon! Troy.' " I rolled my eyes. "He's talking about Ivan," I informed her.

"Your hairdresser?"

"Colorist," I corrected. Picking a calorie-loaded crouton out of my limp salad, I described my brief encounter with the studly cover boy to De. "He was way impressed with my highlights," I concluded.

"Your highlights? Wake up and smell the Clairol, girlfriend," De objected. "That is so not all the buckskin-wearin' babe was impressed with. That hair quiz was just a lame ploy to snag your number. Cher, you are so the props Neve, a youthful Cindy, a Demi unhindered by Bruce and babies."

"Well, yes, but—" I began.

"Let's go the videotape," De urged. "Did you beg the boy for a book? Did you even ask for his autograph? Survey says, 'As if.' Yet did the clever cover hunk manage to get your card? And does he now have your digits? Nod, yes. Plus look at this!"

De pointed to a gold starburst on the cover of *What the Heart Remembers*. "Write a love story in the tradition of Ani K. Niel's romantic bestsellers and win a fabulous dream date with Troy!" it said. "Details in back of book."

"It's a writing contest," I remarked.

"Don't you see," De persisted. "Troy wanted you to have this book. To enter this contest. To win fame, glory, and a righteous all-expenses-paid romantic rendezvous with him."

"You're right," I said, pushing away my plastic salad bowl. "We should have opted for fries."

"How can you talk about food at a time like this?" De demanded.

"Just kidding." I laughingly gave my homey a hug, then picked up the paperback. "Let's check out the contest. How hard could it be to write a love story?"

We turned to the back of the book and were looking over the contest rules when a voice as welcome as Wu-Tang at the Grammys went, "Be still, my heart. Cher is actually reading."

De and I looked up to see the tragedy that was Amber standing beside our table. With her was Sari Strickland, this nasty ninth grader who'd recently started following the tasteless one around.

"Oh, no. It must be a mirage," Sari said, doing a pretty good Amber impersonation. Just like her hair, which the impressionable girl had dyed to match her idol's flaming locks.

At the moment, Sari was trying to hang on to a paper plate full of nachos and cheese while balancing multiple shopping bags and shoe boxes. Most of them, it was safe to assume, were Amber's.

"Nice socks," De remarked, checking out Amber's peppermint-striped thigh highs. "Did you mug Raggedy Ann?"

Actually, in her gaily ruffled blouse and brown Alpine shorts with suspenders, I thought Amber looked more like Heidi getting ready to milk her grandfather's goats.

The redheaded Cruella ignored De's remark. "That's the only literature Cher hasn't listened to since we did the *Ivana Trump Coloring Book* in kindergarten."

"Easy, Amber," De cautioned. "If you tell lies your nose grows back to its original size. Didn't your plastic surgeon warn you?"

"Listened to?" Sari was back at Amber's lame joke, stumped. She set down the plate of nachos, which I have to say looked way tastier than the rabbit food De and I were munching. Malls, even upscale ones, are not famous for fresh produce.

Amber glared at her frizzy-haired fan. "I was referring to the fact that Cher listens to books on tape, Sari. If you can't keep up with my witticisms, find another role model."

"Ouch," said De. "That probably hurt."

"Did not," Sari Strychnine snapped. "Nothing Amber

could say would diminish my admiration for her. Smart, sassy, and furiously self-absorbed, she's my total idol."

"Isn't she cute?" Amber cooed, patting Sari's head as if she were a pet snake. "So what are you reading?" she asked me. "Let me guess, something by Shakespeare that Kenneth Branagh overlooked?"

"As if," Sari added.

"Really," Amber insisted. "I'm dying to know."

"Is that a promise?" De asked hopefully.

"It's Ani Niel's new bestseller," I said, showing them the book.

"Oh, no. Ani K. Niel, the romance writer? Feh!" Amber looked down her surgically enhanced nose at us.

"Anyone can read Ani Niel," Sari said. "She's so easy."

"I think you mean 'trashy,'" Amber corrected her protégé, picking up the book. "I mean, look at that cover."

"Who's the hunk? Is that supposed to be like Troy?" Sari sneered.

"It isn't supposed to be," De said. "It is Troy."

"Cover boy Troy, the monster babe?" Amber asked.

"He's signing autographs in front of the bookstore," I volunteered, "just around the corner."

"Duh, right," the fashion failure said sarcastically. "That is such an obvious attempt to lose us. Like I'd really ever fall for that."

"Yeah. Oooo, Amber, let's hurry to the bookstore. Nice try, Cher," Sari said.

De and I exchanged glances, then burst out laughing. "Look inside the cover," De advised our bewildered visitors. "He just autographed Cher's book."

Sari didn't hesitate. She checked Troy's signature, said, "See you, Amber," and, dumping the pile of packages into Amber's arms, headed out of the food court.

"Sari, wait!" Amber ordered. "I can't carry these. My nails aren't dry yet." She looked around frantically. "You!" Amber shouted to a stupefied boardie. The poor guy had been wandering through the food court like a dazed alien in search of the mother ship.

"Hold these," she commanded. "And if even a single piece of tissue paper is torn when I get back, those dreads you're so proud of are gonna wind up on the south end of a mop where they belong. Do you read me?"

"Er, loud and clear, lady," the stunned boy said as Amber dumped her parcels into his outstretched hands and stalked after Sari.

Chapter 3

*W*hen Dionne phoned me on Monday morning to make sure we weren't wearing the same outfit to school I was practically sobbing.

"Girlfriend," De said, alarmed, "what's wrong? Did you trash your Jeep and incite your dad to threats of allowance reduction?"

"No," I tried to say. But my tear-clogged sinuses changed the word to "Dough."

"Dough?" said De.

I was slumped at my dressing table, still in my powder pink silk pajamas trimmed in white piping. Which even in extreme sadness, I knew looked seriously def. My PJs so went with the warm pinks and creamy whites of my bedroom suite.

"My Jeep's okay," I snuffled, trying to stop crying long enough to apply a decent shmear of creme concealer to my eyes, which were like Panda City from lack of sleep.

"Did you carelessly exceed your credit card limits again?" my bud prodded.

"Well, sure," I said. "But that's not it. It's Ben," I finally blurted. "He died."

"Ben?" De repeated. "Ben, the fish? You named him Ben and then he died. Oh, Cher, I'm so sorry. Please don't hate me. I should never have let you take him home. And Summer, wait till I get my hands on her. Giving someone a goldfish is like giving her the gift of grief and loss. They always wind up floating topside in the tank."

"Ben is not the goldfish, De," I explained, glancing at the cut crystal bowl on my dresser in which the little fish was swimming even as we spoke. "Although, that would be a way props name for him. Ben is Harriet Snowden's honey. Or was. And actually, his real name was Benedetto, but she called him Ben."

"And Harriet is?" De asked, compassion disappearing from her voice faster than a leftover cinnamon bun sitting unguarded on a plate next to Amber.

"Harriet is the tragic yet triumphant young heroine of *What the Heart Remembers*," I said. "Oh, De, Ani Niel is a fiercely outstanding writer. She so knows the adolescent heart. I mean, like, I thought Anonymous, who wrote that poignant poem in last month's *Buzz*, was sensitive," I said, citing one of our school paper's most talked about entries.

"'Blonde Haze,'" De remembered. "That was a righteous poem."

"Well, Ani beats Anonymous hands down," I asserted. "I stayed up all night reading her book. Even

19

though Ben left Harriet a rich woman, I can't stop weeping. I'm way abject, a brutal basket case."

"I call next-ies," De said. "I'll trade you. My mom's got *What the Heart Knows,* which is the sequel to Ani's first million-copy bestseller, *What the Heart Conceals.* So you're saying it's a furious five-Kleenex read?" she asked eagerly.

"You'll need Puffs," I advised, "for gentle lanolin-infused softness. I'm so distraught I can't even get my concealer on, let alone work with a decent lash lengthener. I look like Courtney Love before her Versace do-over."

"So not," De contradicted. "What're you wearing?"

"My pink PJs."

"To school?" she said.

"Hel-*lo,* no. Something blue, I think, to match my mood, in like crushed velvet."

There was a knock at my door. "Cher?" Through the frosted etched glass, I could see Daddy's silhouette. "Cher, which tie goes with my double-breasted Abboud—my striped Sulka or the Holland and Holland print? Oh, and am I supposed to have orange or grapefruit juice today?" Daddy called to me.

I said 'bye to De, blew my nose, and put on a happy face, even though I knew Daddy couldn't see me through the door. As a fully successful litigator—which is the most ruthless kind of lawyer there is—my dad is fiercely independent. But at home he's so cute.

He like majorly depends on my advice and approval. Which of course he fully deserves. I pick out his clothes, oversee his health and nutrition needs, manage the household help, and most important, make him feel needed, like seriously indispensable.

Daddy and I have a very special bond. My mom died

when I was just this adorable infant and sometimes Daddy wonders whether he's enough for me. Which he so is. He's like a mom, a dad, a furiously protective big brother, and an understanding pal all rolled into one. All he wants is my happiness. So I try to be as cheerful as possible around him.

I only resort to tears and pouting when absolutely necessary. Like when I want a slammin' new ensemble or a curfew extension and, out of the blue, Daddy gets all Tough Love and decides that I can't appreciate my truly perfect life unless I hear the moving story of his rise from poverty to prosperity for the gazillionth time.

"Your striped Sulka and half a grapefruit," I advised him through the door.

"Cher?" Daddy put his cheek against the glass. "Are you okay?"

"Duh, of course," I answered, feeling my lower lip quiver unexpectedly.

Daddy came in. He was carrying the ties in question. "Pumpkin, what's wrong?" he asked.

It was no use pretending I was Sarah McLachlan, all upbeat and ready to put together some all-star Lilith Fair. I felt miserable, and Daddy could see right through my faux and trembling grin.

"I just read this touchingly tragic tale of love," I told him. "Lost love. A love so right, and yet it didn't work out."

Daddy nodded. "Sometimes it's like that," he said sympathetically.

I looked up at him. He was smiling at me, yet there was this faraway look in his eye as if he was remembering some poignant moment from his own past. "You mean, like you and Mom?" I asked.

"Oh, no." In his Hermès cotton shirtsleeves, Daddy

sat down on the chaise longue next to my dressing table. "Cher, my relationship with your mother was wonderful. We had you. We were extremely happy together. We made up in quality for what we didn't have in quantity. No, Pumpkin. I was thinking of a time before I met your mother."

"Like when you lived in Brooklyn and were poor?" I said.

"Yes. I was still in high school, just about your age, I guess," Daddy said, "when I met Ina."

"Ina?" I asked, blowing my already raw nose.

"My first true love." Daddy laughed. "I first noticed her in English class. She was a terrific student, used to write poetry. She didn't look like any of the other girls in the neighborhood. She had long, thick, almost wild black hair and intense gray eyes."

"Like Courteney," I mused aloud, "or was she more Julia Louis?" Daddy glanced at me, so without a clue. "Courteney Cox from *Friends* or Julia Louis-Dreyfus, formerly of *Seinfeld*," I explained. "They're your basic raven-haired babes."

"She wore black all the time," he said, as if that cleared it right up. "It seemed very exotic. Kind of mysterious and poetic."

"More Salma Hayek," I noted.

"I was very impressed with that," Daddy continued with this little smile. "The other girls in their bell bottom jeans and tie-dyed shirts and patchwork vests looked gaudy in comparison. Ina Klein. I was crazy about her."

"And?" I prompted him, no longer blue but brutally curious.

Daddy sighed and toyed with the ties. "She was from an extremely well-to-do family," he explained. "Her father was a big-shot lawyer. Very wealthy, very con-

22

nected. Turned out that he was on the board of directors of the company Grandpa worked for. And he did not like the idea of me dating his little girl."

I smiled, thinking of the parade of Baldwins who had called at our Karma Vista Drive casa. The Jeremys and Scotts, the Aldos and Matts whom Daddy had cross-examined and terrorized at our door. "Sounds familiar," I teased.

He blinked at me, all innocent and defensive. "Things are different today," he insisted. "The boys of my generation looked like normal human beings."

As if, I thought. I had seen pictures of Daddy as a high school boy, and I so begged to differ. But I decided not to argue. "So she was this bona fide Betty," I said, moving him along.

I wanted to hear his story. It was so poignant. I mean, Daddy had never even mentioned Ina before. And now this stellar saga of puppy love spilled out of him.

I saw my father as I'd never seen him before. I could totally picture him as a raw-boned Johnny Depp looking across a roomful of Versace-bright babes to discover the single Calvin-clad Kate in the bunch. Only her name was Ina.

She was smart. She was beautiful. She was flipped for him, Daddy said. And she didn't care that his father virtually worked for her father. Against her dad's wishes, they started dating. They rode the subway into the city and introduced each other to new worlds. Daddy took Ina to her first rock concert at the Fillmore East, and she dragged Daddy to poetry readings in Greenwich Village. They ate hot dogs at Katz's Delicatessen on Delancey Street and went for horse and carriage rides through Central Park.

By the time Daddy finished his historical tour of New

York's ancient nightlife, his neckties were practically braided together. He pulled them apart and stood suddenly. "The striped Sulka?"

I nodded. "But, Daddy," I said, "you didn't tell me what happened."

"I wish I knew," he confessed. "One day she said she was going to stay with some cousins in New Jersey for a week. And that was it." He shook out the ties. "Hey, we'd better get going. Don't you have school today?"

"It? Excuse me, what do you mean, 'That was it'?" I demanded.

Daddy shrugged. "I never saw her again," he said. "I tried to find her. Her friends didn't know anything more than I did. Everyone thought she was staying with cousins and was coming back soon. And Ina and I weren't supposed to be dating, so I couldn't just phone her house and ask her parents where she was. I didn't want to get her in trouble."

"That's like so noble," I praised. "Then what did you do?"

"Well, I'd walk past her house every day. You know, hoping to catch a glimpse of her or some clue to her whereabouts," Daddy said. "And then, one day, I went by and my heart sank. The house was empty. They were gone."

My jaw dropped. "That reeks," I remarked.

"It was bad," Daddy agreed. "Boy, I was a mess. I couldn't focus on anything—homework, sports, my afterschool job. I was angry at my parents, too. I blamed them—secretly. I blamed them for not being wealthy, for not being big shots. I almost flunked out of school that year."

"Not even," I blurted. "That is bitterly poignant. So sad."

"It was, in the beginning. But you know what?" Daddy said, his face brightening, suddenly, "That was when I decided to become a lawyer. A big attorney. Bigger and more successful than Ina's father could ever be. And I did it, too. And I met your mother while I was in law school and never looked back."

"So I guess something good came out of it," I said.

"Absolutely," Daddy agreed, gently brushing a wayward strand of freshly shampooed hair back from my forehead. "You."

I leapt up and gave him this monster hug. "That story was so Ani K. Niel, Daddy," I said. "All love, tears, and triumph."

"Ani who?"

"Duh, hel-*lo*. She's only today's number one best-selling romance writer," I explained, walking Daddy to the door. "Half a grapefruit, not grapefruit juice," I reminded him as he headed down the hall.

My desolate mood was so gone. I hit speakerphone and speed dialed De. "Change of plans," I informed her. "Cancel the crushed velvet. It's way too solemn for a Monday morning. I'm doing a glitter-edged turquoise cropped cardigan over my sunshine yellow Mizrahi mini."

"Outstanding," De approved. "I'm in tangerine denim over stretchy plaid leggings."

"Are you doing braids like Saturday?" I queried.

"That was then, this is now," De said. "So, no. Don't forget to feed our fish, girlfriend."

"Who, Ben?" I laughed.

"Are you really going to name him Ben?"

"I'm giving it serious consideration," I admitted. "Don't forget to bring me your mom's Ani Niel novel.

I'm packing my autographed copy of *What the Heart Remembers* right now."

"It's already stuffed in my Ferragamo tote. You sound way recovered, girlfriend," De noted.

"Majorly," I affirmed. "Daddy just told me this torrid tale that rivals Ani's tear-jerking best. It was about this crush he had in his early years that got heinously squished."

"Eew," De went. "Don't you hate it when old people unload their I-was-young-once yarns on you? Especially when they're about bonding. It can be viciously traumatic."

"I know exactly what you mean," I said supportively. "But it wasn't icky like that this morning. It was more like a books-on-tape moment with Daddy reading the story or this excellent flashback scene from a soap episode."

"Whatever," my bud said agreeably. Then she went, "Whoops, I'm Audi! I must've left my hot rollers in too long. My head's all smoking."

Chapter 4

*F*orty-five minutes later, I bounded from my Jeep onto the raked pebbles of Bronson Alcott High School's self-parking lot.

Self-parking is where, mostly, our budget-minded teaching staff stows its secondhand vehicles. Several feet away was the valet parking area. There a certain carrot-topped coed wearing a huge bloodred bow on her head was waiting for an attendant and loudly whining about the lack of service.

"Hi, Amber," I called in passing.

"Eew!" The flamboyant flamehead wrinkled her renovated nose at me. "Why would you park in that ripe used-car lot? Or, excuse me, should I ask, which underpaid teacher are you trying to kiss up to by stashing your wheels in loser land?"

"It's like way more convenient than waiting for

valet service," I replied as two freshman girls shyly approached me.

"Excuse me, we were wondering. Is that def yellow dress a real Anna Sui or just like an awesome copy?" the short Janeane Garofalo–type brunette asked.

"I told you that's Cher Horowitz," her friend, a Heather Locklear blond, hissed. "She would never wear a rip-off. You are Cher, right?"

"Yes, but this buff mini is a Mizrahi. From Isaac's spring collection," I confided.

"Oh, I'm like so embarrassed," the first girl said. "Cher, would you autograph my *Elle?*"

I scribbled my name on her magazine. "That's a slammin' little Gap tee you're wearing. And your friend's Benetton cardigan busts fresh."

"How did you know this was Gap?" the brunette gasped.

"Hel-*lo,* she's Cher," the other one said, whacking her friend on the arm.

"Peace." I raised two fingers in a V and moved along.

Bronson Alcott, the high school I and my popular crew attend, is one of Beverly Hills foremost learning environments. It's like this choice educational theme park, all cleanly landscaped with rolling lawns, graceful fountains, and palm trees so tall that their stately tops practically touch the smog-drenched sky.

Our school owes its manicured acres, spacious classrooms, and cutting-edge sports facilities to the participation of our proud and pushy parents. The Bronson Alcott Parents Association is so powerful that ten out of ten Bronson Alcott graduates go on to college, whether they want to or not.

As I walked across the Quad to the school cafeteria,

with sunlight glinting from the sequined trim of my turquoise cardigan, I could see my true blue waiting for me.

De was sitting at our reserved table on the patio. She was surrounded by an all-star crowd. As I stepped onto the flagstone terrace, the best and the brightest of Bronson Alcott High scrambled to their feet and gave me a standing ovation.

"You really met Troy?" Baez, our bud of the peroxided pixie and multiple jangle bracelets and piercings, called out as I approached. "And he personally autographed a book for you? I'm like dying."

At De's proud nod, I pulled the paperback out of my backpack and handed it to Baez. "See what he wrote," De prompted. " 'I'll call you soon.' "

"Troy is going to call you? Get outta town!" shrieked Alana, the Minnie Driver–haired daughter of a famous New York newscaster. "How amazingly gorgeous is he in real life?"

"Studly is an understatement," De volunteered.

"Was he dressed as a knight, a rogue, or a cowboy?" Janet, our crew's Asian-American overachiever, wanted to know. In addition to being a brutal babe, Janet's IQ so soars.

"He was in buckskin and leather," I answered.

A chorus of sighs and squeals broke out as I slid into the seat next to De that her main boo, Murray, had vacated for me.

"A chair for the Cher," Murray announced, giving me a dimpled grin that radically stretched the little line of fuzz on his upper lip which the boy so proudly called a mustache.

Despite De's best efforts to upgrade Murray's wardrobe, her tall, dark high school honey was in standard boy wear: humongous unlaced sneakers, baggy Phat Farm jeans, a knee-length XXL Stussy shirt, and a backward Kangol cap with the price tag hanging off it.

"Buckskin and leather?" Sean, Murray's best friend and hat-wearin' homey, made a sour face. "That is so whack," he said, shaking his head—which made the dreadlocks attached to his red, yellow, and black Jamaican knit cap waggle like a nest of hairy snakes. "Why would a guy wanna dress up in a costume?"

Jesse Fiegenhut glanced up from the *Rolling Stone* he was browsing. Two skinny old wrinkled guys were on the cover. "It's different if you're Liv Tyler's father and you've been wearing platform boots and weird makeup since the seventies," he declared.

"Is that Liv's dad on the cover?" I asked.

"Liv's dad is the lead singer for Aerosmith," Jesse sneered at me, which he'd been doing off and on since I turned him down for a date in like eighth grade. "The golden oldies on the cover are Mick Jagger and Keith Richards."

Although Jesse was exceptionally gifted in the looks arena, his personality basically blew. He owed his A-list status to the fact that his father, who was a music industry mogul, could snag front-row freebies to the most monster concert events of our day.

"Whoever they are they look way older than my dad," Alana said.

Nathan Kahakalau, the transfer hottie from Hawaii's Kalani High, shrugged. He was zipped into this rubberized wetsuit jacket, accessorized with baggy Gotcha surfin' shorts and red flip-flops.

"Haoles be strange," Nathan observed.

"Ha-what?" Baez asked.

"*Haole* is the Hawaiian word for 'Caucasian,'" Ringo Farbstein, Janet's Einstein-esque boyfriend, translated. "I hear you, bro," he said to Nathan, and they slapped five.

"Yo, so, Cher, straight up." Murray struck this muscle beach pose. Flexing his Stussy-draped arm, he flashed me a huge toothy smile. "That cover dude ain't fresher than me, right?" he said.

"Oh, please." De scornfully studied her man's generic attire. "Stale bagels are fresher than you in that whack outfit. Wake up and smell Neiman-Marcus, Murray," she snapped, casually tossing back her long dark hair, which looked excellent and utterly unharmed by her hot roller mishap.

"Ooooo," said Ryder Hubbard, who had skateboarded up to our table. "She dissed you, man."

"What happened to your head, Ryder?" Baez asked, turning toward him with a clatter of bracelets and earrings.

Ryder's shoulder-length locks, which normally looked as if they'd been conditioned with Crisco, were brightly streaked with various colors.

"What, this?" he asked, selecting a greenly tinted tuft from among his red, blue, and purple striped follicles. "Summer was testing hair wands on me yesterday."

"You were with Summer yesterday?" De asked Ryder, then she gave me this surprised look that said, Hello, did you know about this?

I shrugged and shook my head no.

"Yeah," said the burnt-out boardie. "I was like rollin' past this makeup place on Rodeo Drive, eyeing a parking meter, thinkin' about maybe going for it—I mean, like grabbing some air and hotdoggin' over the money machine—when Summer saw me through the window and like ran out and snagged me for her evil experiment."

"Oh, so it was a chance encounter, not a date," De said.

"So not a date," Summer confirmed, joining us at the table.

De and I quickly examined her thick auburn hair for signs of a bad color wanding. Gratefully, we found none.

"Spotting Ryder on Rodeo was a total freak accident," Summer continued, "as, I'm sure, is Amber's upcoming rendezvous with the cover hunk."

There was this sudden silence at our table. You could have heard a Sprint pin drop. For a moment the only noise was the snorting laughter of an amused cyber-geek sitting at the end of the patio known as Outer Nerdgolia.

De and I exchanged glances. Mine was like, Can Summer be referring to Amber Marins and my Troy toy? And De's was all, Not even!

"Amber has a what with who?" Alana demanded.

"Whom," Janet Hong corrected her, then spun toward Summer. "By cover hunk you don't mean Troy, do you?"

"Excuse me!" De held up a pause finger, which had been excellently French manicured. "Summer, are you insinuating that Amber has somehow scored a date with cover boy Troy? Cher's Troy?" she added loyally.

"That's what Sari Strychnine said," Summer gently replied.

"Oh, you mean that little Cruella in training who's been trailing Amber lately?" Baez lowered her cropped platinum head and peered over her Bada shades at Summer.

"I just ran into her on the latte line," Summer said, setting down her tofu danish and soy milk. "She says Amber's prepping for a dream date with Troy."

The morning pretty well bit after that.

Word of Amber's close encounter with the cover boy spread through school like the Hong Kong chicken flu.

Frantic fans would pass me in the hallway and be all, "Way to go, Cher. I heard you got Troy's autograph." Then faster than Linda Evangelista changes hair color, someone else would go, "Yuh, but Amber snagged a date with the world-class hottie."

A dream date with Troy. The phrase stuck with me as I moved through my A.M. classes in a daze.

Was it possible that Troy, whose emerald green eyes had so gazed into mine, whose tanned manly fingertips had toyed with my hair, whose flagrant full lips had asked for my hairdresser's name, would become suddenly crushed on Amber?

Sari claimed it was true. Amber's pint-size shadow bumped into me between classes.

"Ouch!" I cried, as her steel-toed Doc Martens stubbed my strappy sandaled feet.

"Well, excuse me, your Cherness," she blurted. "I guess you've heard the four-one-one on that hunka, hunka burnin' love, Troy, and my idol, Amber."

I nodded distractedly. It was hard to listen to the girl. Particularly when I was noticing how wrong the swampy green of her polyester ensemble looked with her frizzy, newly red hair.

"I bet their dream date is gonna be harder for you to swallow than vegetarian chopped liver," Sari crowed.

"Sari, gloating is so unattractive," I said. "Plus, if you're going to wear green, go toward the brighter shades. I'd so stay away from muddy hues. Actually, you ought to let De and me do your color chart."

"My color chart?" The girl peered up at me suspiciously. "Oh, I get it," she said, her thin mouth curling into a cold smile. "Amber warned me about you. She said you'd try to get on my good side. Well, forget about it," Sari warned. "I don't have one."

"Whatever," I said, making the *W* sign with my fingers. "Have a nice day."

"Have a nice day?" Sari repeated sarcastically. "I bet you wear Smurf pajamas," she called after me.

Ignoring her, I hurried to English, my last class before lunch. I cellularly speed-dialed De on the way.

"You know all this stuff about Amber's dream date," I said the minute she answered.

"Hel-*lo,* I've been hung up on that phrase since this morning," De confessed. "Dream date. Familiar, isn't it?"

"Are you thinking what I'm thinking?" I asked. Turning the corner, I could see De heading my way.

"If what you're thinking," she said, with a foxy grin, "is that Amber doesn't actually have a date with the blond bombshell."

"Exactly. But she thinks she can get one by entering and acing the romance writing contest." I clicked off cellular and went person to person. "And she just happened to state her hopes for the future in the present tense," I continued our mutual thought as we met outside English class.

"Bingo!" My plaidly clad bud snapped shut her Motorola and took my arm. "Amber doesn't have a lock on Troy. She barely has a prayer. While the girl has been known to grind out a lame cheer now and then, a parody of poetry, even a partially plagiarized essay, in order to win Ani Niel's contest she'll have to really write a love story."

"All by herself," I added as we entered Mr. Stanky's room.

Chapter 5

*O*ur gray-bearded, ponytailed English teacher, Mr. Stanky, was at his desk. He acknowledged my cheery hello with this bored grunt. His face, I noticed, was looking kind of yellow, and he had these pumpkin-colored creases at the corners of his eyes.

"Mr. Stanky's tanning gel's gone rancid on him again," De noted.

"I know." I sighed. "I tried to tell him last time to check the expiration date."

A flash of light momentarily blinded me. I squinted and found it was coming from the back of the room, near the windows.

There, upholstered in this tacky patent leather tube dress that showed an icky surplus of freckled skin, was Sari's scary sponsor, Amber.

Sunlight glinted off the bloodred fabric of her high-gloss costume, which so resembled a shiny, extra-wide belt. The huge matching hair bow that I had noted in the parking lot topped off the outfit. It too was made of patent leather. It stood up stiffly on Amber's head, giving her this Mouseketeer Madonna look.

The immaterial girl was engaged in intense conversation with the boy who had given me his seat at the food court on Saturday.

Brandon was his name, I recalled. He was all tall and rumpled looking, wearing wrinkled chinos and a washed-out corduroy shirt under a vintage U.S. Army jacket.

All huddled in front of the windows, Amber was whispering and gesturing and rolling her heavily made-up eyes, which looked as if they'd been accented with a burnt twig.

Brandon seemed way intrigued with her monologue. He listened intently while toying with the fully props petite hair tuft tucked between his lip and chin.

As he stroked his facial follicles, I couldn't help but notice how the boy's gleaming dark locks fell forward over his forehead. He kept flipping back his hair with a toss of his head while Amber gushed and murmured.

Greeting friends along the way, De and I moved toward our seats. They were located near enough to Amber and Brandon for me to hear the leather-girdled one say, "So I want like a really, really romantic totally tear-your-heart-out tale, in five thousand words or less, neatly double-spaced."

"No problem," Brandon responded.

I couldn't believe it. It was like, hold the pickles, hold the lettuce. Amber was ordering a prize-winning love story, well done!

The bell rang. Brandon and Amber took their seats.

"Did you hear that?" I asked De as Mr. Stanky

banged his ruler on the desk in this pathetic plea for attention.

Everyone was all into their pre-class warm-up activities.

Racing their remote control Hot Wheels, Murray and Sean were making crashing and exploding noises as their mini vehicles buzzed through the aisles.

You could hear bad cuts from a Squirrel Nut Zippers CD erupting through Jesse's headphones. Sharon the grunge queen was grooving to the leaked sounds while swabbing the new safety-pin hole in her nose with an antibacterial salve.

Bracelets clanging, Baez was massaging a conditioning relaxer into Alana's full-bodied locks.

"Amber is plotting to cheat her way to the top," I told De just as the class settled down and this embarrassing silence fell on the room.

Before De could comment, Mr. Stanky went, "Cher, would you care to share that with the entire class?"

"No thanks," I went, and plopped down into my seat.

While Stanky ranted about some homework paper that had come in covered with what he hoped was dried egg, I pulled out *What the Heart Wants*. I hid De's mom's book behind my spiral-bound and started reading it.

By the time Ryder confessed that the soiled paper was his and that the mystery gunk on it was either axle grease from his new board trucks or a flattened wad of banana bubble gum he thought he'd stuck behind his ear on Saturday and had been looking for ever since, I had read the first chapter and was bitterly engrossed.

Ani Niel was an excellent writer. In a way, I found myself wishing that she had been at the mall that day. I mean, Troy was a true gorgeoso. No doubt. He was the face, pecs, lats, and abs of perfection. But the real star was Ani. She was the brains. It would have been the bomb to meet her, I mused. Which was actually, I suddenly remembered, one of the contest prizes.

I skipped to the back of the book to find out more about the talented babe. The author biography just said that she'd written fourteen novels, won a couple of awards, and currently lived in Southern California.

I got all caught up in the story again. When the bell rang, I didn't even look up. I would have stayed there reading all day if De hadn't roused me.

"Snack time, girlfriend. You coming?"

Reluctantly, I closed the book and gathered up my things.

"Hel-*lo*, was that the most boring thirty-seven minutes ever?" my bud asked.

"I was totally entranced," I said.

"Girl, you're postal. Today's session was seriously Sominex."

"Oh, you mean English." I saw my error as we headed out of class. "I was talking about your mom's book. De, it's like a full-out major must-read."

"I'm going to start on *What the Heart Remembers* tonight," she pledged. "So what were you saying about Amber before Mr. Stanky so dimly interrupted us?"

It took me a moment to leave Ani land and re-enter earth's atmosphere. "Amber?" I went, and then I remembered. "I think she's trying to get that kid Brandon to do her dirty work."

"What, like annoy, aggravate, and insult people?" De

asked as we cruised through the hallways waving to fans and nodding and blowing kisses.

"No, to write the love story," I said. "For the contest."

We pushed through the main doors and stepped out into the sunshine of the quad. Frisbees were flying. Boardies were performing kick flips and ollies over the benches bordering the walks. Sunbathing slackers littered the lawn. It was lunchtime.

"Why would she do that?" De said, outraged.

"To win?" I suggested.

De slapped her flawless forehead. "Well, duh. I guess. What I mean is, why would Amber try to get that wonk Brandon to write her entry?"

"Because," Summer said, sidling between us, "the boy is a bona fide poet. Didn't you catch his opus in the *Bronson Buzz* last month?"

"Was that the piece on why we need more ATMs on campus?" De asked, "or the impassioned plea to have Starbucks cater the cafeteria?"

A chill ran up my yoga-stretched spine and hit me right between the chakras. Suddenly, I knew what Summer was talking about. I stopped in my tracks and turned to face her. "You mean that fierce poem by Anonymous?"

Summer nodded. "Wasn't it the bomb? Brandon wrote it. I saw him working on it in Stanky's class like a week before it hit the school paper."

"Get out!" De said, stunned. "Willy the wonk wrote 'Blonde Haze'?"

"Ask him," Summer said as we approached the cafeteria. "He's right over there. On the patio. With Amber."

They were planted at our regular table. The patent-leathered one was picking sweet potato fries off Brandon's plate as he skimmed a copy of *What the Heart Remembers*. It was the book with Troy's clinch on the cover.

Even as De and I stared, Baez, Janet, and Ringo crossed the patio, carrying their trays over to join Amber and her partner in plagiarism.

"What are we going to do?" De wanted to know as we walked toward the table.

"Well, we could point out that cheating is wrong," Summer suggested.

"Oh, that would really work," De went. "Not."

"De's right," I gently told Summer. "Remember, we're dealing with the girl who wrote 'Where Have All the Orthodontists Gone?'"

"And when Mr. Stanky noticed how similar it was to Paula Cole's 'Where Have All the Cowboys Gone?', Amber claimed Paula ripped her off," De reminded us.

"Actually," I said, "I'm not like absolutely sure that Amber and Brandon cut a deal."

"Well, if it isn't the autograph seekers," Amber said loudly as we dropped our backpacks onto the bench. "Did you stop by for mine? It will so increase in value when my winning love story, accompanied by a picture of Troy and me on our dream date, gets published in *Romance Digest*."

Brandon looked up and saw me. This epic grin spread across his minorly bearded, poetically props face. "Hi, Cher. Take my seat," he said, starting to get up.

"Oh, no. There's plenty of room. I'll just scooch in here between Janet and Baez," I said.

Amber looked from me to Brandon and back again. "You two know each other?" she asked suspiciously.

"Everyone knows Cher," the boy said, all starry eyed and smiling.

I picked up Amber's copy of *What the Heart Remembers,* which he'd been looking at. "So, are you a fan of Ani Niel's?" I asked him.

"Actually, I'm just browsing to get a feel for her style," Brandon replied. "I've never read a romance novel. But so far, yeah, she's not bad. A lot better than I thought."

"Isn't she?" I agreed. "I mean, this guy at the mall gave me a copy—"

"By this guy, she means Troy," De added. "By the way, Amber, what did he write in your book?"

" 'Good luck,' " Brandon said. "Wasn't that it?" he asked Amber.

I turned to the front of the book. There was Troy's big, bold script. Brandon was right. "Good luck" was all the coverboy had scrawled above his signature.

"That's just because we got there late." Sari, in her reptile green slip dress, slithered up to the table carrying a tray of cafeteria goodies. "And like Troy was already gone. So we snagged a presigned book off his chunky assistant."

Amber shot Sari this evil look.

"Whoops," said the clonette. "All I'm sayin' is if Troy had been there he would have inscribed a way more intimate message. Right, Amber?"

"Vacuum pack it, Sari," Amber ordered.

"Eew, are those hamburgers?" Summer paled as Sari set down her tray. "How can you eat beef?"

"Put a sock in it, Oprah," Sari snapped, whirling at her. "Do you know how many polyesters died for this dress? But you don't hear me whining about it, do you?"

"They're probably veggie burgers," I tried to reassure the shaken Summer.

De patted our distraught friend's shoulder. Then she crossed her tangerine-denimed arms and turned her attention to Amber, who was unloading the pineapple pizza from Sari's tray.

"So let me get this straight, Amber," De said. "You never actually met Troy. Which would mean that probably he didn't ask you out. Which further implies you have no dream date with the studly boy at all."

Janet, Baez, and Ringo had stopped gorging. Mouths agape, forks stalled, they were watching us. Their eyes followed the action like dazzled tennis spectators at the U.S. Open.

"Is that basically it?" De pressured Amber.

"Excuse me, but I personally never said I had a date with the ferocious Fabio," she protested, sounding about as convincing as Pinocchio. "Although, count on it, I will."

"You told me you did," Sari blurted.

"Hello, are you contradicting me?" Amber thundered at her protégée. "You who were a ninth-grade nothing when I found you? You who thought you had what it took to become even a flawed copy of me? You who I've tried to help, shape, mold, teach—"

"You said you were going on a dream date with Troy," Sari sullenly insisted.

"Going," Amber pointed out, "implies a negotiation in progress, not a done deal, my little Judas. And I am going on that date, the moment my poignant tale of romance wins the contest."

"*Your* tale?" I said. "Or Brandon's?"

"Brandon's?" Janet asked as all eyes swung toward

43

the poet formerly known as Anonymous. "Are you entering the contest, too?" she asked him.

"Well, some of the prizes look pretty good," the boy said with a laugh. "I could use the cash, dictionary, and library of classics. And, actually, I wouldn't mind meeting Ani Niel. But no. I'm not entering the contest, I'm just going to write the story."

"For who, Amber?" Baez asked. "But that's unfair. I cry foul. You can't do that, Amber."

"Excuse me. What I can't do is windows," Amber snarled. "Also floors, laundry, and pool maintenance. I don't cook my own meals, either. Hel-*lo*, we hire help. It's just our way of life. And what could be more natural than for me to continue a totally choice family tradition?"

"You're not doing this for money, are you?" I asked Brandon.

Before he could answer, Sari went, "Oh, right, like there'd really be a high school student in the entire 90210 zip that needs a financial boost. Wake up and smell the stockbrokers, Cher."

"No, I'm not doing it for the money," Brandon told me. "I'm doing it for a chance to meet Harold Shomsky. Amber promised to introduce me to him."

"Harold Shomsky, the mail-order steak king?" De asked, perplexed.

"You're thinking of Henry Chumpkin," Ringo corrected De, "the butcher of Bel Air. Harold Shomsky is one of America's greatest living poets."

"As if," said Baez. "Like Amber would really know a literary legend like what's-his-name?"

"Shomsky," said Brandon.

"Oh, Baez, you're so right," Amber crooned. "Or at least you would be if Harold Shomsky were not a pathetic, viciously neurotic Barney who sees my father, the eminent Beverly Hills psychiatrist, Dr. Marins, like five days a week!"

"Amber!" Ringo gasped. "You're not supposed to tell anyone who your father's patients are. It's confidential information. You're not even supposed to know! That's a breach of professional ethics."

"Ethics, shmethics," Amber grumbled. "If it'll get me a dream date with a cupcake like Troy, who cares?"

I looked at De. She was furious. "I don't believe you," she barked at Amber just as Murray and Sean wandered over.

Sean was still sporting his Rasta cap with the dreads attached. "Did someone say cupcake?" he asked, greedily surveying the table.

De glared at the boy buds.

"What?" Murray said, noting her distress. "I didn't even do anything yet. I didn't say anything. Why you looking at me like that?" he whimpered.

"It's Amber," De explained. "She's cheating."

"On who?" Murray asked.

"Okay," De said in this dangerous voice, "Now it's you."

"Congratulations, bro," said Sean. "We've been here a total of two seconds. I think you just set a new world record for buggin' your boo."

"Oh, I get it. I get it," Sari suddenly announced. "You're jealous. That's what's wrong." She was staring right at me.

"Jealous?" I said, deeply bewildered.

"You're jealous of Amber," Sari blustered. "You're just not creative enough to come up with a way to win on your own, Cher. So, of course, you resent my mentor's innovative approach."

"Innovative?" De said dryly, "Like, see under: lying, stealing, and cheating."

"Sticks and stones may break my bones," Amber recited, pausing her pizza pigout to make the *W* sign, "but when your dad is as prominent an M.D. as mine, you can always find excellent orthopedic surgeons. So . . . whatever," she said.

"Not creative enough?" Summer challenged Sari. "Cher's got more creativity, imagination, and talent in her peerlessly manicured little finger than some people have in their whole insensitive beef-eating bodies," she said with sudden passion.

"I second that emotion," De added.

"Cher knows teen angst," Baez blurted. "If she wanted to, she could tell like the most buff story of bummed-out adolescent romance ever."

Suddenly, everyone was staring at me. Which, of course, I'm way used to. Only like, at the moment, they were waiting for me to respond.

Usually that is so not a problem. I'm very spontaneous and rarely think about what I'm saying. But, I have to admit, I was just a smidge unsure of myself. Not unsure, like insecure or anything. More like undecided.

If I *was* going to enter the contest, it wasn't going to be because of Amber or her evil twin.

I glanced at the book lying between Brandon and me. There on the jacket was Troy, the well-toned, blemish-free, most-wanted cover boy in America. Swept up in his arms was this slender yet fiery Barbie in crinolines who, if I wrote an awesomely amorous love story, could so easily be me.

It would be clean to hang with a famous hunk like Troy.

"So, girlfriend," De prodded, all psyched, "are you

going to write the book of love and snag that dream date?"

I looked up and my eyes met Brandon's. The dark-haired young poet, who reminded me of like Ethan Hawke and Matt Damon and Ben Affleck and all the adorable wannabe award-winning writers in L.A., was smiling at me. He was waiting for my answer, too.

"I don't know," I confessed. "It's like a major maybe."

Chapter 6

*T*o enter the romance writing contest or not to enter the romance writing contest?

I spent an hour after school fretfully pacing my spacious room, as heinously perplexed as Hamlet. Only a nine-one-one call from Alana snapped me out of my muddle. The girl was in dire distress.

In the pantry of her mom's Holmby Hills mansion, Alana had found a shopping bag from some random discount store. It had been tucked away among the choice Bloomie's, Saks, and Nordstrom bags.

Was her family keeping something from her, the abject Betty wanted to know. Had they lost a bundle in the stock market or, worse, lost their sense of style?

Alana was viciously freaked. "Why would my mom be shopping in a budget boutique?" she demanded.

My heart went out to her.

"Girlfriend, once they leave the store, shopping bags

take on a life of their own," I advised her. "Daddy once brought home a T.J. Maxx bag, and I had the exact same reaction as you. I brutally panicked. I thought he'd blown some major case and that we'd have to switch from sparkling Perrier to Poland Spring water. But the shopping bag turned out to be filled with law books that Daddy had schlepped home from the office. It had come from his secretary's daughter's babysitter, who shops in the Valley."

"I hope you're right," Alana whimpered.

"Count on it," I said.

Which worked out really well. Since it turned out that the bag Alana had discovered actually belonged to her housekeeper's mother's maid. And my own harsh dilemma was unexpectedly solved the next day.

I was finishing up Ani's book in Mr. Stanky's class. It was either that or risk dozing at my desk like everyone else.

The Stankster himself, wearing his favorite suit—a shoddy designer knockoff that was so totally made in China there was still rice on the lapel—was standing in front of the blackboard.

He was mumbling about the dysfunctional home life of the Brontë sisters, Emily and Charlotte.

Charlotte Brontë's popular classic, *Jane Eyre,* had been published in 1847, he said, turning to scrawl the date on the board.

I only half-listened after that. Everyone in the class had Cliffs Notes on the saga anyway.

And Murray was sitting behind me, snoring. De's hibernating honey was so loud, she had to pinch him to quiet him down. But Stanky droned on, oblivious.

"Mmmdowha?" Murray murmured.

"Shhh," De warned him. "You were snoring and like keeping me awake."

"You woke me to tell me I woke you?" Murray asked, all grumpy.

"Are you up, De?" I whispered.

"Is this class over?" she asked.

"As if," Murray grumbled. "We'll be at the cineplex, buying senior citizen discount tickets to the premiere of *Scream 200* before Stanky winds up this lecture."

"Eew," De went. "You're drooling."

"Guys do that when they sleep," Sean drowsily informed her.

"Real guys," Murray added.

"Dat's da haps," Nathan confirmed, without lifting his long-haired head off his desk.

"De," I said, "I'm almost finished with *What the Heart Knows*. Does your mom have *What the Heart Conceals?*"

"Whew, girlfriend. You're jetting through those volumes," she noted.

"It's such stirring reading," I enthused, "you just don't want to stop. It keeps you way more awake than some of Bronson Alcott's illustrious teaching staff."

"Like who?" De said, laughing. "The Big Pumpkin?"

"It's so sad," I mused. "You'd think a teacher would be halfway decent at learning. But, hel-*lo*, how many times can you tell a man to can the tanning gel, lose the beard and ponytail, put some Grecian Formula on his dull gray locks, and splurge on one serious suit?"

"Watch out!" a voice behind us hissed.

"Big whoops," De said as Mr. Stanky's shadow fell across my desk.

"May I assume that you're reading a Brontë classic, Miss Horowitz?" he snapped, snatching De's mom's book from the center of my spiral-bound.

Suddenly, Summer raised her hand. "Excuse me, Mr. Stanky," she called out.

Stanky glanced over his shoulder at her. "Is that graffiti on your hand?" he asked, squinting at Summer's henna tattoos.

She quickly withdrew her digits. "It's not permanent. It's done with natural dyes," she said defensively. "But anyway, it's Ms."

"Ms.?" Stanky stared at Summer. Everyone was waking up and like groaning and rubbing their eyes. "Thank you for offering us that pithy feminist perspective, O defender of all things great and small."

Summer got all red and embarrassed, but she stood her ground. "It's just way more politically correct to say Ms., not Miss," she asserted.

"It's okay. Just call me Cher?" I suggested.

"Or Mud," Amber piped up. "I mean, after you get a look at what she's reading, that's what her name will be anyway, right?"

"Oh, what a surprise," the ponytailed prof said sarcastically, as he flipped through the book's pages on the way back to his desk. "Why, this isn't by Charlotte Brontë at all. Nor is it by her esteemed sister Emily.

He turned the book toward the class so that everyone could see the cover. All the boys hooted and groaned. The girls went, "Be still, my heart, it's Troy. He is so the bomb."

"In fact, people," Mr. Stanky sneered suddenly, "this is not literature at all. It's trash."

"Oh, and like that imitation Armani you're wearing isn't?" Amber muttered.

Everyone else was all, "Ooooo, he said the *T* word."

I leapt to my feet, which were adorably encased in these fun chartreuse Hush Puppies that looked phenomenally phat with my lilac pedal pushers and matching short-sleeved cashmere crewneck.

"I object, Mr. Stanky," I called out. "How can you, a molder of fragile young minds, so demean a book? Like, excuse me, but shouldn't you be encouraging reading, not disparaging reading material?"

"Translation!" Ryder had awakened.

"What Cher said," a voice behind me explained to the sleepy skateboarder, "is that it's basically a teacher's job to support, not suppress, literature."

I turned and saw that it was Brandon who had so smoothly simplified my point of view. I gave the boy a full-out grateful smile.

"Literature?" Mr. Stanky's artificially tinted face flushed from mellow yellow to like chili-pepper red. "I'm surprised at you, Brandon," he said bitterly. "This is a romance novel. A cardboard-bound soap opera. Are you really defending this insignificant little love story as literature? I thought you had better taste."

"Taste?" I heard Amber say. "I call your attention to the man's suit again."

"Actually," Brandon said, pulling Amber's copy of *What the Heart Remembers* out of his jacket pocket, "I'm reading Ani K. Niel's novel, too." With that the epic Ethan marched up to Stanky's desk and tossed down the book.

As Mr. Stanky reached for the book, Amber yelled, "If you so much as crinkle one page of that passionate paperback, which is personally autographed to me, I'll have you embroiled in the lawsuit of your life, buster!"

"Hel-*lo*. Excuse me. Mr. Stanky," I called out again. "Would you call *Jane Eyre* literature?"

"Not only do *I* call it literature," the teacher replied

with major attitude, "it is universally acknowledged to be a classic."

"Subtitles!" Ryder cried again.

"What part?" Janet, our black-haired brainer bud, asked the struggling slacker.

"University of Knowledge, I think," he said.

"Universally acknowledged," Janet said helpfully, "means, like, 'Everyone agrees.'"

"So like, if I say the book is rank, then it's not universally acknowledged anymore?"

"Sit down, Ryder," Stanky ordered.

"Mr. Stanky, isn't *Jane Eyre* a romance?" I asked. "I mean, isn't it a kind of Jurassic soap opera about this fresh yet penniless orphan who had to support herself in a world that was way unfriendly to people without wealth and powerful connections, let alone penniless orphaned girls?"

"And in those days," De said, scrambling to her feet, "there was practically nothing girls were allowed to do. I mean, you couldn't even flip burgers because this was radically pre-McD."

"Like forget a military career," Summer chimed in. "They never even heard of the Equal Rights Amendment in that dark age."

"So the only career path a props Betty could find was working as an au pair," I continued. "Which Jane did. She became a governess in the home of a mysterious hottie named Mr. Rochester, who had a daughter in desperate need of nurturing."

"And they lived on this spacious yet weird estate," De said.

"Did it have its own private zoo," Murray ventured, "like Neverland?"

"Excuse me?" De's hands flew to her slender hips, and she pinned her honey with a wilting stare. "Is it your cap that's on backward or your head?" she asked. "Hel-*lo*. We're talking about Mr. Rochester, not Michael Jackson."

"Anyway," I moved along, "Jane falls for Rochester, who's a gazillionaire, and he's like all crushed on her, and they're getting set to bond in wedded bliss when Jane discovers her honey has a terminally postal wife stashed in the attic."

"Get out," Baez said, all shocked. "That is so *One Life to Live*."

"Exactly," I agreed. "Only it's *Jane Eyre*. So what I'm saying, Mr. Stanky, is that just because a book is about love and romance doesn't mean it's trash."

"Shakespeare's *Romeo and Juliet* was about young love," Baez offered.

"And so was *The Hunchback of Notre Dame*," Sean shouted.

"A Disney classic," Murray backed his big.

"Which was written by Victor Hugo," Brandon added, "the author of *Les Misérables*."

"*Les Mis!* Was that a fabby show or what?" Alana demanded. "My father, the famous network anchorman, snagged us two on the aisle for the Broadway extravaganza when I was in New York last spring, per my parents' bitterly complicated joint custody agreement."

"My dad could've gotten you better seats," Jesse said.

"Mr. Stanky, I recently skimmed that Ani Niel book I gave you." Brandon pointed to the novel he'd tossed onto the front desk. "And some of the plot elements reminded me of *Anna Karenina*, Tolstoy's moving masterpiece of love and loss."

"You're comparing Ani K. Niel to Count Leo Tolstoy?"

As the stunned teacher picked up the novel and began flipping through it, I glanced over my shoulder at Brandon.

The props poet threw me this excellent wink. Which, I have to say, I returned in kind without even worrying about whether my lash extender would flake. Standing tall and slim in his fatigue jacket and faded jeans, the brilliant boy looked even better than he sounded.

"In conclusion, Mr. Stanky," I announced, recharged by Brandon's stellar support, "one man's trash is another man's Tolstoy!"

There was this monster burst of applause from my fellow classmates accented by piercing whistles of approval.

"People! Settle down, people!" Mr. Stanky called out. Then when the room was as quiet as it was going to get, he said, "That was very well done, Cher."

My buds began to cheer again, but Stanky dumped cold water on their warm enthusiasm. It took him only two words: "Your assignment," he said. And everyone started groaning and grumbling and throwing wadded-up paper and smacking their foreheads.

"No, no. This is going to be fun," Stanky insisted. "We're going to enter a writing contest."

Startled, I looked over at De. My bud shrugged, as surprised as I was.

"We who?" Murray inquired.

"We *you*," our teacher replied. "All of you. I was going to assign this measly little one-page essay on the Brontës' contribution to early nineteenth-century literature. But that was before I discovered your interest in the romance genre."

"Uh-oh," Sean murmured. "I'm getting a bad vibe here."

"So, using the literary principles learned in this class," Mr. Stanky continued, "each of you is going to compose an original five-thousand-word love story to submit to Ms. Ani K. Niel."

"Over my liposuctioned body!" Amber leapt to her feet. "I've already commissioned a winning romance tale."

"Fine," said Stanky. "Then your homework assignment is practically complete."

"I don't want to win a dream date with somebody who looks like Arnold Schwarzenegger," Sean protested.

"My father can fix you up with Marilyn Manson," Jesse name-dropped.

"I don't want to come up with a five-thousand-word any kind of thing," Murray carped. "I like that one-pager option. Measly, I think you called it, Mr. Stanky, sir? Measly works for me."

"This is so your fault, Cher," Amber hissed.

"Do something," Sean pleaded.

De grabbed my hand and squeezed it supportively. "Pass the low-fat spread, girlfriend," she whispered. "We're toast."

"Not even," I protested.

A rumble of grumbles swept the room. I bit my lip and concentrated with all my might, seeking a solution to the whack turn of events. And then I jumped up from my seat again.

"Gosh, Mr. Stanky," I said, giving him my most sympathetic smile. "I so admire your work ethic. I mean, there are more than twenty kids in this class—"

"Twenty-six, to be exact," Janet offered.

"And if each of us writes a five-thousand-word story, well, that means you'll have to read . . ." I paused and turned to Janet's brainer boy toy, Ringo.

"A hefty one hundred and thirty thousand words," the brainer boy instantly obliged.

"Few of which will be properly spelled and/or legible," De pointed out, "especially if everyone's computer crashes at once and we have to like handwrite these yarns."

"Yuh, I'm thinking maybe I'll do mine in felt tip, you know. Aw, but that like leaks through from one side of the paper to the other and it gets so hard to read," Baez said with this mischievous grin. "Ooo, I know. I'll write it in crayon, with like illustrations!"

"Cool. You could do smiley faces all over the page, right?" Ryder was warming to the task.

Mr. Stanky's head was swiveling. As he tried to keep up with the comments around the room, his smug smile so faded.

"Mr. Stanky, I have a suggestion," I volunteered.

He turned to me, looking hopeful.

"What if our entire class worked together on one story," I suggested.

"You mean collaborate on this assignment?" Stanky asked.

"Sure, like those reporters who wrote *All the President's Men*," Murray said enthusiastically.

"Bernstein and Woodward," Ringo filled in the names.

"Or Canfield, Hansen, and Kirberger," Summer called out, "who wrote *Chicken Soup for the Teenage Soul.*"

"Or Caswell and Massey," Alana suggested.

"They do soap," Amber snapped, with surplus attitude.

"So?" Alana said.

"We could start out with three teams," I announced, giving De a work-with-me-girlfriend look.

"And each team would come up with a dope love story." My bud knew right where I was going.

"And then we could all choose which one we like best." Summer began to get the idea.

"And that would be the one," I emphasized the word *one*, "which we would all work on together and make awesomely excellent and enter in the contest."

Mr. Stanky mulled over the notion. "And that would be one five-thousand-word story I'd have to read," he reasoned.

"Which I'd volunteer to edit," Brandon said.

"And I'd proof for spelling and grammar," Janet added.

"And Cher could be in charge of the whole project," De announced excitedly.

"And everyone can send her their story ideas, and she'll pick out the best one," Summer added.

"We're talking about three different teams coming up with story suggestions," I reminded my overly enthusiastic friends.

"Well, you should head one of them," Alana said.

"I can do that," I allowed.

"And after the class selects the most totally props tale of all, my best will whip it into contest-winning shape," De declared.

"Dionne!" I began, but Summer drowned out my protest.

"I'm on Cher's team," she called as Stanky wrote my name on the blackboard. "And we're way open to ideas. I mean everyone feel free to forward their story notions to Cher, okay?"

"Any other volunteers?" Mr. Stanky called out. "If this cockeyed idea is going to work, we need two more team leaders."

Cringing in their seats, my classmates were suddenly all engrossed in their textbooks and trying desperately to avoid eye contact with our ginger-hued teacher.

Unexpectedly, Ryder raised his hand.

"You've got it, Mr. Hubbard," Stanky declared. Whirling around, he scrawled Ryder's name next to mine on the board.

"Got what?" Ryder was asking everyone. "I was just gonna say I don't think *Jane Eyre* is all that rank."

"Well, now you're heading up a story-writing team," Baez informed the startled slacker.

"Me?" Ryder shook his shampoo-hungry head in disbelief. "Whew, dudes, I'm like speechless. About a second ago, I was all, if I don't say something nice about Jane, my grade in this class will radically blow. And now you honor me in this ultimate way. My fellow dudes, I'll do my best."

"That boy is shedding brain cells faster than dandruff," Amber said.

"Ms. Marins, did I hear you volunteer?" Mr. Stanky challenged.

"If you did, that thatch of hair in your ears must be seriously in need of thinning," Amber barked. Then she put on a grin not seen since the last shark scare off Malibu. "While I'm a natural leader, unfortunately, Mr. Stanky, I'm allergic to group activities. Cooperation makes my skin break out. So, while I'd really like to join your little class project, I'm afraid it's a health risk I'll have to pass up."

"Not this time," Stanky said firmly. And he added Amber's name to the list.

The bell rang.

"That's it for today!" Mr. Stanky shouted. "Captains, you can form your committees on your own time. This will be a collaborative class project. We'll all be working toward one double-spaced, spell-checked, easy-to-read, contest-ready romantic tale. Cher, my hat's off to you!"

"Well, get a haircut or put it back on," Amber grumbled.

Chapter 7

"**H**ere's another one about a girl whose wicked stepsisters dress in Badgley Mischka and force her to wear their mom's old Diane Von Furstenberg wrap dress to the ball," De said.

We were crashed out in my room. I was sitting crosslegged on my pink brocade bedspread, sorting through stacks of story suggestions. De was sitting in front of my power PC, checking my E-mail. Pages of computer printouts littered the plush carpeting of my sumptuous suite.

"Is there a slipper involved?" I asked.

It was two days since my bud had blurted out her blond suggestion that I head up the class project, and my fax machine was still grinding out strange scenarios.

"Duh, yes, specially designed by Ferragamo," De reported.

The fax was beeping again. "See what's coming in, De," I said. "Oh, and thanks again for volunteering—me."

"Face it, girlfriend, you were so the logical choice," my true blue insisted as the downstairs chimes went off, signaling yet another parent, chauffeur, or messenger service delivering more story ideas from our unstoppably creative classmates.

"Cher!" Daddy bellowed from below. "There's a gypsy here to see you."

De and I looked at each other, then nodded. "Summer," we agreed.

"She's wearing her Peruvian poncho, bet?" I said.

"With huarache sandals and healing crystal necklace," De guessed.

From the mess of papers on my bed, I gathered up the pile of possibles. "We'll be right down, Daddy. Thanks," I called.

"I'm leaving now," he shouted. "What do you want me to do with her?"

"Let her in, Daddy. It's just our friend Summer," I explained. "You met her parents during open-school week."

"What about Cinderella Von Furstenburg?" De asked.

"Dionne, it's like the twentieth Cinderella variation we've received."

"Right." She tapped the keyboard. "Whoops, I hit delete."

Summer knocked on the door, then stuck her head into the room. "Wow," she said. "What happened in here? It's looks like El Niño blew through an Office Depot megastore."

"Excuse me," I said, "are you the same Summer who

suggested everyone in class forward their whack ideas to me?"

"Bummer," Summer said. "Well, anyway, I took care of the treats. They're here. I saw the catering truck pulling away as I drove up."

"Excellent," I said, glancing at my Swatch. "The rest of the committee should be here soon."

"Oh, is that my fishy?" Summer cooed, hurrying over to the dresser.

As Summer peered into Ben's bowl, De gave me this panicked look. "I didn't know Summer was ordering the snacks," she said. "Her idea of fun food is a carrot muffin and a carafe of designer spring water. We'll starve to death."

"It'll be fine," I promised, grabbing my copy of *What the Heart Remembers*.

"Are you sure you're not overfeeding Ben?" Summer asked. "He looks way plumper than he did on Saturday."

"You see," De whispered.

"I hope Whole Foods sent enough stuff," Summer said as we thundered down the graceful white marble staircase.

"Me, too," De said. "I'm way overdue for my après-school snack."

We headed to the kitchen where the humongous tray Summer had ordered was sitting on the stainless steel utility table.

"What did you get?" De asked as Summer removed layers of brightly colored cellophane from the tray.

"Oh, you know, the usual yummies," our planet-saving friend said, dramatically unveiling the platter. "Salt-free veggie chips, carrot sticks, kiwi slices, oat

63

bran pretzels, succotash salsa. I think that's every-thing.''

"That's it?'' De said. "That's all?''

"Summer,'' I asked, gently, "what about people whose food consciousness isn't all that evolved?''

"Who, like boys?'' she said.

"Well, yuh,'' De said. "I mean, Murray, Sean, and Nathan are part of our story-selection crew, too.''

Summer looked distressed. "Well, I got lemon-flavored, low-sodium mineral water, too,'' she said, meekly.

"It's an extremely healthful treat platter, Summer,'' I tried to console her.

"Why don't you just schlepp it into the den, while Cher and I gather some supplementary snacks,'' De suggested, handing Summer the tray.

"Just in case someone's dehyrated and needs salt,'' I explained as Summer started toward the door.

"Or wants to be able to identify what they're chewing by taste,'' De added when Summer was gone.

De pulled out her Motorola slimline. "Murray can pick up some stuff on the way over,'' she said, hitting speed-dial. "I'm thinking Oreos, taco chips, pizza. Hello!'' she said, trying to get my attention. I was idly gazing at the cover of my book. "Can you think of anything else?''

"I'm okay with pizza and kiwi slices,'' I said, tearing my eyes from the buff golden-haired bodybuilder on the cover and quickly flipping to the contest rules in the back of the book.

"Excuse me, but how right was I about Summer's snacks?'' De said, getting off the phone.

"So right,'' I acknowledged, "and yet so wrong about Troy.''

"Girlfriend." De hurried to me and took my hands. "You're not brooding because the babe hasn't beeped you yet, are you?"

"Brooding? As if," I said. "I was just thinking it'd be clean to see the humongous hottie again, that's all."

"Count on it," my best pledged, giving me a heartening hug. "He'll call."

"He *was* kind of noble at the mall. All interested in me and like who did my highlights." I shrugged philosophically. "But who has time to brood, girlfriend, let alone sulk, pout, fret, or dwell on? We've got stacks of ripe story suggestions to review."

"Here's a cool one," Sean said about an hour later, waving a FedEx from our classmate Tiffany, the daughter of Dr. Gelfin, Murray's family dentist. Having annihilated the pizza and Oreos, we were arrayed around my den, reluctantly scarfing Summer's treats.

"We already read the one from Tiffany," Baez objected. She, Nathan, and Alana were sifting through the last of the faxes. "'Jakob Dylan and the Dentist's Beautiful Daughter,' right?"

"Naw, this is a different one." Sean bit into one of Summer's salt-free oat bran pretzels. His face heinously pruned.

"Do not even think about hurling," De warned him. "Swallow and read."

Sean handed the paper to Murray, grabbed a napkin, and lunged out of the room.

"'Luke Perry and the Dentist's Exceptional Daughter,'" Murray began. "'Once upon a time . . .'"

"Trash it," Alana ordered. "Cher, I don't think I can listen to one more ill tale. They're all egregiously dumb fantasies or fairy-tale rip-offs."

"We need something romantic yet real," Summer agreed. "I mean, something you can believe for a hot minute."

"I can believe Tiffany Gelfin and Luke Perry," Baez said. "I wouldn't necessarily want to read about it, but Luke's not all that booked right now."

"What would work is a sweeping saga of love about real people, young people just like us," I said.

De agreed. "An epic yarn that expresses the raw emotional truths of Bettys with credit cards, cell phones, and attitude."

"Kids with way more clothes, cars, homes, and parents than they know what to do with," said Baez, whose mom had been married five times, including once to Janet Hong's father.

"I wish Brandon were here," I said, surprising myself. "He's so good at writing."

A picture of the tall, lanky teen poet popped into my mind—Brandon scrambling from his food-court chair, all smiley faced and respectful.

I could just see his dark, glossy locks falling forward and the way he pitched back his head to get them out of his eyes, which were this mossy brown shade, not quite green but choice.

And, of course, that petite follicle patch in the middle of his strong chin. Would it feel silken or scratchy during a smooch, I found myself wondering.

"Conflict of interest," De said, rousing me from my reverie. "Brandon's already working on Amber's entry. The boy is bitterly psyched about meeting that Shomsky guy."

"But he's on for editing our story once we get it down on paper," Murray said.

Alana started pacing. "Young love. Young and strong and brave."

"And yet doomed," Summer suggested. "I mean, like so right and yet crushingly thwarted."

"But with a happy ending," Murray insisted.

"Eh, brah, how 'bout this?" Nathan hauled himself up off the antique Aubusson carpet in front of the fireplace, where faux flames were leaping. "A surfer dude from Oahu like rides this fierce tube," he said, tossing back his blond-streaked black hair, "and then he like scores big with cool freebies from his sponsors, like these excellent T-shirts from Piko and wetsuits from Four-X."

"Yeah. I'm with you so far, man," Murray said.

Nathan threw his arms wide and started nodding his head. "It's solid, right?"

"But then what happens?" Baez prompted the boy.

Nathan shrugged. "I don't know. That's as far as I got."

Sean returned from his unscheduled flight. "Wassup?" he asked. Everyone was staring slack-jawed at Nathan.

"Well, at least it was original." Summer slumped back into Daddy's favorite burgundy-leather club chair.

"That was a very nice start, Nathan," I agreed. "But we need a love interest."

"Like maybe the surfer boy gets wiped out," Murray suggested.

"Yeah." Sean got right in on it. "And then this Pamela Anderson–looking babe has to swim out in this fierce storm to rescue him, and it's pouring down, and lightning is flashing, and he's like all thrashing in the water."

"No wipeouts," Nathan declared suddenly. "This guy's too good. I'm withdrawing my story."

There was a lull. The only sound we heard was the lonely crunch of Alana biting into a beet chip.

"What about you and Murray?" Summer turned enthusiastically to De. "I mean, you guys have a tale of young love to tell."

De glanced at her Hilfiger-draped honey. This smile of remembrance crept over her chronic face. "Well, it started at Penguins," she said softly. "Murray was getting this double-scoop waffle cone—"

"Humphrey Yogurt," Murray said.

"It wasn't Humphrey Yogurt. Although Humphrey's has the totally ultimate yogurt," De acknowledged.

"Humphrey Yogurt," Murray insisted. "I didn't even go to Penguins till after I met you. You and Cher are all that over Penguins, but they don't mix no fruit there. The flavors are whack—"

"You lie," De said.

"Dionne, it doesn't matter," I tried to interrupt them. But they were all into their *Soul Food* thing, snapping on each other like Nia and Mekhi. My only hope was to distract them.

"Hey," I went, all loud and cheery, "Daddy told me this ferocious love story that actually happened—"

It worked. Sort of. Everyone started going "Eew" and "Yuck" and "Don't even go there."

Murray and De both turned toward me. "Parents aren't supposed to be tellin' you stuff like that," Murray said.

"My man speaks the truth," Sean affirmed.

"Your dad told you this story?" Alana said. "I thought our fable was going to be about the young and the restless."

"But it is," I said. "I mean, it takes place during high school."

"Yeah, but it's your dad's story, and he's old," Baez protested.

Summer started waving her hand. "Compromise," she called. "Like maybe this could be a story about what happened to two really young people, but then they grow up and run into each other again all these years later in like a retirement condo in Laguna Beach."

"Oh, right," Alana cut in, sarcastically. "And he's a photographer and she wears these boring K-mart aprons. I mean, hello, what're we writing here, *The Bridges of Orange County?*"

"I didn't say it was about Daddy," I asserted, fudging the facts just a smidge. "I just said he told it to me."

"Did it happen to one of his clients?" Nathan asked, warming to the possibilities. "And like now they're in this really harsh lawsuit where's she's trying to take him for every cent he's got, and he's threatening to chainsaw their house in half or something?"

"Shhhh," De said. "Let Cher tell her story."

So I did. Basically.

But I decided to update the names from Mel and Ina to Neve and Jason.

And I dropped the Brooklyn setting because it was way retro.

And I changed the mean father from a lawyer to the ruthless head of a communications conglomerate that published influential supermarket tabloids and produced shows like *Extra* and *ET* that could crush careers in a heartbeat merely by showing these heinously unflattering pictures of prominent people.

And I added this romantic touch: Jason had given

Neve a ring just before she left for Ibiza, which was where I said her cousin lived. Ibiza is this fabulous resort island in the Mediterranean. It sounded way cleaner than New Jersey.

Anyway, my buds were seriously spellbound. All you could hear besides my voice was dry food being crunched and once, after someone made the mistake of dipping something into Summer's succotash salsa, this momentary gagging sound.

"And he never saw her again," I concluded.

My buds were watching me, glassy eyed.

"Well, that's it," I added.

"Not even," Baez protested. "Where did Neve go? What happened to her? Did she find a new love or like pine for Jason to the end of her days?"

"Well, at least she had the ring," Alana said sullenly. "I mean, I'm assuming it was a good one. Even though he didn't have a lot of money, he wouldn't have given a girl like Neve some chintzy little costume jewelry ring."

"Not even!" Summer was annoyed at the suggestion. "Jason was so sensitive and so much in love. It was probably this valuable family heirloom, like from his grandmother, maybe. Five carats or better, I'm guessin'."

"Oooo, so his granny is loaded, right?" Sean said. "Like she's got megabucks stashed."

"If we want her to be," De said all of a sudden. "That's the fun part. We're writing the story, so we can make up whatever we want."

"Cool," Nathan agreed. "Let's make her Granny Rose from *Titanic*. And instead of the ring it's that necklace."

"Oh, yeah." Murray started pacing excitedly. "And

she didn't dump it overboard, right? She gave it to her granddaughter—"

"Grandson," Sean reminded us. "I like the ring better. Granny's real old and rich, and she gives this ring to Jason from her very own gnarled and aged hand."

"And he gave it to Neve the night before she disappeared," Baez said.

My crew was so stirred. These viciously inspired ideas were being aired around the room. Then a telephone started ringing, and everyone scrambled for their cellulars.

I checked mine and motioned to my buds. "It's okay, it's for me," I said, then I went, "Hello, yes, this is Cher Horowitz."

Everyone got right back into discussing the story. Then the front-door chimes started clanging. I couldn't hear the person on the phone. "I'm sorry," I said, putting my free hand over my ear. "Someone answer the door, please," I urged.

"I'll get it," De volunteered. She turned to go and suddenly I heard my caller clearly.

I reached out and grabbed De's sleeve. When she saw my expression, her eyes went all boing!

"Get the door, Murray," she ordered, staring at me and mouthing, "Him! Is it him?"

"Oh, hi, Troy," I said, nodding yes to De.

Alana, Baez, and Summer started screaming.

De glared at them, stifling their ecstatic cries, though they kept jumping up and down hugging each other. Then my best bud tried to get her ear next to the phone, and our shapely cheekbones collided with a monster crack.

"Yeow!" De bellowed.

"Ouch," I blurted.

"Who's on the phone?" Murray asked, returning to the room.

"Troy," De said. "Who's at the door?"

"Brandon," he replied.

Chapter 8

*D*id he ask you out?" a group of giggling girls squealed as I crossed the Quad to class the next day.

"Is he as heroic as he looks?" Ms. Hanratty wanted to know when I bumped into her in the hall outside algebra.

"Are you sure it was him, and not some vengeful, hoax-playing stooge trying to humiliate you because you think you're so gorgeous and popular and act like you're all that?" Sari demanded, cornering me at my locker.

In less than twenty-four hours, all of Bronson Alcott knew that cover-boy Troy had personally phoned my Beverly Hills maisonette.

They didn't have the details down. They didn't know that the hottie heartthrob had called to thank me for giving him my colorist's digits.

Not that that was all we talked about.

Troy also told me how his agent and publicity person loved his new highlights. And that his makeup man had spent half an hour trying to guess who'd done the streaks. And that he hoped I didn't mind but the photographer who was supposed to shoot his next cover was so freaked by how outstanding his locks looked that Troy had actually given him Ivan's number.

I was all, "No problem. I'm glad it worked out."

So "Troy called Cher" was the total dish du jour at school, the buzz of Bronson Alcott. But no one knew how strangely psyched I'd been to see Brandon, in his wrinkled T-shirt, big schleppy army jacket, and XL-size chinos, sauntering into my den.

He'd just finished outlining Amber's story, he said, and thought he'd stop by to see how we were doing, and whether he could help out.

It was a stellar act of do-goodism. My posse positively pounced on the charitable babe. While I was on the phone, getting the four-one-one on Troy's hairdo, De and the gang enthusiastically recited our tale to Brandon.

The boy was way encouraging and jumped right in with all these radical recommendations of his own. He particularly liked the part about the keepsake ring and gave me this choice thumbs-up sign when De told him that it had been my idea.

By the time I clicked off the Troy call, Daddy was pulling into our circular, cobblestoned driveway. Everyone decided it was time to scatter. So, basically, I spent about two whole minutes with Brandon and hardly got to say anything but "It was chronic of you to come by. See ya."

Now, as I headed toward English class with De, I saw him coming toward us down the hall. Amber, in a neon blue ballerina gown and ponyhide cowboy boots, was scurrying alongside him, her mouth doing ninety in a twenty-five mile zone.

"But Amber's got to be taller than the guy," she was saying. "I mean, as the heroine of my saga, shouldn't she dominate?"

"I still don't think we should call her Amber," Brandon responded. "Not that it isn't a fresh name," he added tactfully, "but do you really want a story by, for, and about Amber Marins?"

"Duh, let me see, does 'You got that right, buster' express it best? That is exactly what I want," the ego that ate L.A. responded.

"It could get confusing to your readers," Brandon cautioned.

"Then they'll just have to stretch, won't they?" Amber asserted.

"Whatever." The boy laughed. Then he noticed me. "Hi," he said, with this moving, melt-your-heart smile. "Are you all set for your presentation?" he asked when we were almost at Mr. Stanky's door.

"Got my notes right here," I said, waving my pink clipboard at the helpful honey.

"Poor, Cher." Amber blinked her goopy lashes at me. "I heard you so forced youself on Troy at the mall that my dream date broke down and gave you a pity call. The boy is so easily manipulated," she said, "but I like that in a man." Then, trailing layers of loud blue tulle, she swept past us into the classroom.

"Didn't we see that costume in *The Nutcracker* last Christmas?" I asked De.

"Yeah," my bud said, "when Amber played the nut."

"Classic casting," I noted. We gave each other a high

five and followed the ballistic ballerina into Mr. Stanky's room.

After attendance, our tangerine teacher told everyone to put away their Walkmans, Watchmans, CD players, makeup, hair accessories, teen 'zines, virtual pets, laptops, and lollypops. "All right, let's start with committee updates," he said. "Ryder, did you work out your love story?"

"Whoa, dude." Ryder got furiously flustered. "I'm not even seeing anyone."

"Call EMS, I'm in shock," Baez murmured. "Ryder, he means the story you and your crew came up with for the contest."

"Oh, wow." The boardie seemed way relieved. "That weirded me out. I thought you were getting into personal stuff, and I was like, whoa, wassup with the tanning-gel man, that dude's getting dangerous—"

"Excuse me?" Mr. Stanky's florid face darkened. "What did you call me?"

Ryder blinked cluelessly. "What? Like . . . a dude? Is that what you mean?"

"I believe he called you tanning-gel man," Amber helpfully explained.

"Put a sock in it, Amber," De growled. "Ryder, who else is on your committee?"

"Hey, like whoever," the boardie responded. "Anyone who wants to be. Any takers?" he asked, scanning the class.

"What you're saying, Mr. Hubbard," Stanky said, "is that you are unprepared."

"For what?" Ryder went.

"Sit down," Stanky snapped. "Amber, I trust you've overcome your aversion to group activities—or are you

76

ready to receive the same low end of the alphabet grade Mr. Hubbard is going to get?"

Amber stood in a cloud of scratchy blue tulle. "Dream on, wage slave," she announced, flouncing up the aisle with an envelope in her hand, which she slapped into Mr. Stanky's palm.

"What is this?" the red-faced teacher demanded.

"A note from my family doctor. Read it and weep. It confirms my strange yet serious disability. That allergy to working with others that I told you about."

"But it's written on a page of your father's prescription pad," Mr. Stanky noted.

"Hello, did you happen to notice the M.D. behind my daddy's name?"

"Amber, this is unacceptable," Mr. Stanky said with barely controlled rage.

"Oh, and your taste in clothing isn't?" Amber went.

Everyone gasped. The mass intake of breath was so severe it practically suctioned the beard off Mr. Stanky's frighteningly flushed face.

"He's not my favorite instructor, but he doesn't deserve to die like this," De whispered to me.

"We've got to do something to stop the slaughter," I agreed. "Mr. Stanky, Mr. Stanky!" I started waving my hand.

"I don't want to hear it!" the agitated English meister yelled.

"Back off, Cher," Murray advised. "That vein in his neck is getting ready to blow."

"Mr. Stanky, my committee would like to make its presentation," I persisted.

"Oh, yeah, but what? What's the catch?" he snarled. "You left it in the limo this morning?"

"Actually, it's right here." I raised my pink clipboard. "I and my team are totally prepared."

"You are?" Stanky said.

"Entirely," I assured him.

For a second I thought the shock might finish him off. His eyes got all misty, but he just nodded gratefully. "Sit down, Amber," he said in this hoarse voice.

As the queen of mean returned to her seat, I stood and brushed a speck of lint from my hot pink Prada pedal pushers, which flawlessly matched my stretchy sleeveless top.

There was the usual outpouring of admiration and affection from my peers. I waited until the whistling and stomping died down. Then, clutching my clipboard, I walked to the front of the room.

"We've got a ferociously golden story, and it is so the winner," I announced, standing in front of Mr. Stanky's desk. "I want to thank my chronic committee for the excellent job they did."

Of course, everyone started cheering again. Sean, who was wearing a big knit beret with this powder blue pom-pom on top, was loudest of all.

I nodded appreciatively, then cleared my throat. "I'd like to thank De, who's been there for me since grade school," I continued, "my always supportive best."

Murray leapt to his feet and led the applause for De.

"And to express my gratitude to Murray, Sean, and Nathan, of course," I smiled radiantly at my boy buds, "for their creative, manly input."

"We put the flava to the mix! Wait'll you hear this story," Sean declare with a gusto that set his pom-pom wobbling. "I'm the one who said the granny should be rich," he confided. "It was such a phat move. I'm so psyched."

"You sure you don't mean psycho?" Murray whipped off his straw golf cap and whacked his bud's shoulder. "You're carrying on like the Prozac poster boy. Let Cher finish," he counseled.

"And to Baez and Alana—and, of course, Summer," I summarized, "for catering the session so adequately with oat bran pretzels and succotash salsa."

"Is that what that was?" Murray asked De, wrinkling his nose so hard that his boyish 'stache got all puckered.

"Excuse me. Mr. Stanky!" It was Amber again. "Is this ceremony going to wind down soon? I've got a dermatologist appointment sometime before the millennium."

"Coarse pores?" Baez asked.

"Actually," I said, "I was just about to launch into the tale. It's about this poor boy named Jason—"

"Poor?" Paroudasm Banefshein, the son of a gazillionaire oil mogul, snickered. And, of course, his whole Porsche-driving Persian posse joined in. "Is that poor as in pitiful or poor as in poverty?" he asked.

"Hello, is there a difference?" Tiffany went.

"Duh," Parou said irritably, twisting the diamond encrusted flexible band of his solid gold Rolex. "Absolutely. I have to be able to relate to the hero."

"Then we'll make him pitiful," Nathan said.

A low rumble of Farsi insults greeted the Hawaiian hottie's suggestion.

"Actually, Jason's family has been caught up in this whack corporate merger," I improvised. "His dad's company got downsized in a hostile takeover, and management heinously slashed his salary."

"All righty then," the Persian prince said. "I can live with that."

"Okay, so," I continued, "Jason, the victim of cutbacks that have thrown his home life into chaos, is actually brutally bright. So we know from the beginning that the boy's financial future is secure. He is definitely going places and will be able to offer some lucky Betty a monster prenuptial package someday."

"But for now," De picked up the story, "he's just this unbelievable Baldwin, a totally to-die-for hottie who's still in high school—"

"Public or private?" Janet inquired, mindlessly winding a glossy black lock of hair around her fiercely French manicured fingers.

Everyone turned to stare at her. The Einsteinette stopped twirling her follicles, shrugged, and went, "I'm just curious."

"No problem," I assured her. "I'm open to suggestions."

Ryder's hand flew up. I felt sure he was going to ask for a hall pass, but the boardie surprised me. "Well, if his pops got swamped by the forces of evil—" he began.

"I object!" the other Tiffany, Tiffany Fukashima, jumped to her feet. "Are you calling a savvy CEO, a chief executive who runs a monster corporation that snaps up its smaller, badly run, practically bankrupt competitors at bargain prices, evil?"

"Tiffany," I tried to calm the irate Betty, "Ryder doesn't even know your dad."

"Naw, whew, no way would I diss anyone's dad," Ryder insisted. "That's harsh. I was just thinking the Jason dude might not have tuition for private school, that's all."

"But he's really, really smart," Baez reminded everyone. "So he could get a scholarship if he wanted."

"Hel-*lo!* Who cares?" Alana got all grouchy. "Can we move on, please? Let's get to the goodies. Cher, tell them about our sassy heroine, Neve."

"I think it should be a private school," Summer blurted. "One of those really strict sleepaway academies in some spooky old mansion, like the orphanage Jane Eyre was in."

"That would be a def atmospheric touch," I agreed.

"But orphanages back then were like public schools now," De pointed out. "Bronson Alcott excepted, of course."

"Why don't we vote on it?" Mr. Stanky suggested, looking up from Jesse's father's copy of *Rolling Stone,* which he'd confiscated earlier in the week. It was the issue with Mick and Keith on the cover.

The whole thing was so *X-Files.* First that a gray-bearded teacher was even browsing the 'zine. But also, that he looked like a baby compared to the aged rockers on the cover.

Anyway, Mr. Stanky set down his reading material and took a vote.

It was eleven for public school; thirteen for private, with two people abstaining: Jesse, who was plugged into his CD player, grooving to Black Flag, and hadn't heard the roll call; and Amber, who was busy snapping Polaroid author photos of herself and couldn't be bothered.

After we voted, I got into the chronic heart of our story.

Everyone flipped for the character of Neve right away. Although there was some serious discussion about whether she had to wear black all the time. We finally agreed that it would be way more fun to dress her up in

Anna Sui and Guess? and Mizrahi and a generally brighter and more varied palette. You can be poetic without being grim, we all agreed.

By the time I got to the part where Jason discovers that Neve's family has moved away, everyone was so into the story that people started booing and hissing.

"Not even!" Annabelle Gutterman shouted with a catch in her throat.

"How low can you go?" Ryder grieved.

"Well, at least she got a decent five-carat ring off him before they parted," Tiffany G. noted.

"So then what happens?" Brittany wanted to know.

"That's when Jason decides to become richer and more powerful than Neve's dad," De said.

"Straight up," Murray added, "The bro soars to stardom like Babyface."

"Jason takes over Neve's dad's corporation and replaces the heartless CEO with his own father," I explained.

"Which is when we move forward to the present day," Summer said.

"Neve has become a big poet under another name," Alana revealed.

"Because she's so burned at what her dad did," I told my enthralled classmates, "She doesn't want to use her family name anymore. Not where it really matters to her, like in her famous poems."

"So she calls herself . . . get this"—Sean was twitching with excitement—"Nosaj Neerg!"

"Eeew!" many of our peers shrieked.

"Naw, naw, don't you get it?" Murray went. "It's Jason Green spelled backward. She took Jason's name, not just his ring."

There was a burst of applause from the Persian section. "Nosaj is a beautiful name," Paroudasm declared.

"Okay, so one of the big companies Jason now heads up," I continued, "happens to be the book company that publishes Nosaj's choice poetry."

The class frantically approved that turn of events. There was this hum of grateful murmurs as they began to see a happy ending in sight.

"Yeah, and kids all over the country are reading poetry," Summer enthused, "because Nosaj Neerg writes about the things that really rock them."

"Like that true love has a way longer shelf life than Tough Love," De asserted.

Amber did this exaggerated yawn. "Ooops, I'm sorry. I totally forgot my toothbrush," she said, "So I guess I won't be able to stay for the rest of the pajama party. Hello, can we bring down the curtain on this overstuffed turkey? Dot the *i* in over? How does the forlorn loser discover his long-lost love?"

"Oooo, you're gonna love this." Sean was all hyper again.

"Jason has a copy of Nosaj's recent bestseller right on his shelf," I explained. "And one morning, while he's shaving, he sees the book in the mirror and, hel-*lo*, her backward name is frontward and he massively gets it!"

"And Jason would have bookshelves in his bathroom because . . . ?" Amber grinched.

"Duh, because he's rich and sensitive and he loves reading and can have bookshelves anywhere he wants them!" Alana snarled.

There was this massive outbreak of accolades and applause, which Mr. Stanky had a tough time halting.

"Remarkable. That was quite a story." Our recovered teacher orangely glowed with pride. "I think everyone agrees that you've done an outstanding job, Cher."

"I couldn't have done it without my humongously helpful true blues," I noted, graciously sharing the spotlight.

Amber leapt to her cowhide-booted feet. "Don't even think about reciting that stooge roster again," she warned. "I have a pedicure scheduled right after my skin doctor, and then I'm doing a spin class at S.E.T.S. so I can be flawlessly toned for my date with the cover doll."

"Does everyone agree that Cher should now write the story she just outlined?" Stanky asked, basically ignoring the bonehead outburst.

"Totally!" the class responded.

Brandon, all rumpled and writerly and brutally beaming, volunteered to work closely with me. To the cheers of our peers, I accepted the chronic poet's clean offer.

Then De kicked off this grass-roots movement to make me the designated dater. "The torrid tale of Neve and Jason was basically Cher's idea," she reminded the class. And everyone in the room, except a certain bitter ballerina, so agreed that when, not if, our entry won the contest, I would be the lucky Betty to collect first prize—the dream date with Troy!

Chapter 9

It was the best weekend. Beyond fresh. I never knew writing could be so *fun*-damental. What actually made it frapp was sharing the burden with Brandon.

He showed up at my door early Saturday, toting his laptop. He was decked out in his everyday shabby-chic. Yet there was something so laundered in the lanky boy's look. His buff hair was shower-fresh, and the crisp smell of Tide rose off his wrinkled Army surplus jacket.

Unfortunately, Daddy got to the door before I did. He was blocking the entrance, giving Brandon a talk about insulting the uniform of the U.S. military when I came bounding down the stairs.

"You kids." Daddy shook his salt-and-pepper-haired head at my classmate. "That jacket, it's a joke to you, isn't it? Just something to wear. Like those moronic pants that are ten sizes too big."

"Hey, Brandon." I peeked out from behind Daddy and waved. "I guess you two have met?"

The pale poet was speechless. His lips were so limp they practically hid the mad soul patch on his chin.

"Hi, Daddy," I said, reaching up to buzz Daddy's stubbly Saturday-morning cheek. "This is Brandon. He's a monster writer. We're working on a school project together. Brandon, this is Daddy, who *People* magazine once called 'the pitbull of the Appellate Court.'"

"Morning, Pumpkin." Daddy nodded distractedly, then got back to his lecture. "You kids, you go out and spend a couple of bucks at an Army-Navy surplus store—"

"Not even," I interrupted. "A couple of bucks barely feeds the parking meters on Melrose. Vintage clothes are wickedly pricey."

Brandon blinked at me.

"That's even worse," Daddy said. "You spend your parents' hard-earned cash—"

"As if," I mumbled. "Like the shops in this town would even recognize U.S. currency if they saw it. Beverly Hills is so credit card, Daddy."

"Did you ever ask yourself— What's your name? What's his name again?" Daddy asked me when Brandon's mouth moved but no words were forthcoming.

"Brandon," I prompted. "And he's an excellent student, Daddy. At least in English his GPA is brutally props."

"Well, Brandon, did you ever ask yourself whose jacket you're wearing? Do you know anything about the guy, the soldier boy, the raw, scared, brave kid who once wore it?" Daddy was on a roll. You could see his legal training coming out like blades on a Swiss army knife. "Do you know what he went through? The hardships he endured, the sacrifice and sorrow, the friends he made and the innocence he lost?"

Brandon cleared his throat. "Well, um, yeah," he kind of croaked.

"Really?" Daddy was caught by surprise.

"It's my grandfather's," Brandon said, pointing to the faintly visible name stenciled on the camouflage fabric. "Actually, I've written two poems about him and his Vietnam experiences. One of them won a prize from this veterans' organization."

"Mel Horowitz," Daddy said. For a second, I thought he was going to salute. Instead, he extended his hand, which Brandon cautiously shook, and we all went inside.

Daddy had a golf game scheduled. And although he now seemed less judgmental of Brandon, he made it clear we weren't going to hang home alone while he was out.

Brandon and I looked at each other, like, Okay, now what? I went, "Well, it's way too warm and sunny to hide in the library or even collaborate over lattes at Barnes and Noble. Where can we work?"

"Malibu?" the brilliant boy suggested.

So while Daddy and Brandon got better acquainted in the library and made small talk about what Daddy would do to him if he caused me the slightest grief, I packed up my clipboard, slipped into a chronic Cacharel swimsuit from Everything But Water, and got set for a grueling day at the beach.

We drove in our separate but equally excellent road vehicles to Topanga Canyon State Beach, where catamarans and windsurfers were bouncing on the sparkling sea and the occasional playful dolphin dove between them.

Brandon pointed to this little oasis at the far end of

the rocky shore. We took off our shoes and walked toward it along the edge of the water, getting our toes wet on the way.

"Where do we start?" I said after we'd spread out our tatami mats in front of a dune shaded by tall tufts of beach grass.

"How about the outline?" Brandon asked, taking his laptop out of its case. "You brought it, didn't you?"

"On diskette and hard copy," I bragged. "Duh, how blond do you think I am?" I started fishing around in the huge straw beach bag I'd gotten as a bonus gift for buying a ton of L'Oréal at Macy's. "It's in here somewhere, along with my towel, bottled water, collagen-enriched natural protein moisturizing sunscreen, and Daddy's marbled Mont Blanc pen."

The boy was kneeling on his mat, concentrating on setting up his PC. I found the diskette and held it out to him, but he was oblivious.

"Mont Blanc is a serious writing tool," I said. Then, when he still didn't look up, I murmured, "It makes you write like John Grisham."

That got his attention. "John Grisham writes with a Mont Blanc?" He glanced over at me and took the disk.

"Probably not while cranking out *The Client* or *The Firm* or whatever," I improvised wildly. "He probably used a computer for that. But I bet he's all Mont Blanc when he's signing the contracts for his multimillion-dollar book deals."

My poetic partner studied me for a moment, then grinned. "In answer to your earlier question. Very," he said.

"Excuse me?" I pulled my clipboard with the outline on it out of my bag.

"I was answering your first question," he said, all straight-faced.

I thought back. "Not even!" I yelped. "You think I'm blond?" I tossed my clipboard at him.

He caught it cleanly and laughed. "Your hair," he quickly denied the diss. "I just meant your hair."

"Right, like you just noticed."

"Cher," he said, quietly, "I've been noticing you for quite a while."

I looked at the boy, expecting to see him smiling. But he wasn't.

His mossy brown eyes held mine, and there was something serious in them, I mean, in addition to these green, almost golden flecks lighting the brown.

"I can't believe we've been in the same English class for months and I never really got to know you," I said, softly.

"Well, one, I transferred into Stanky's class late in the term. And two, I'm way better at writing than talking. And three, my camouflage jacket," Brandon said, still in eye-lock mode.

"What about your camouflage jacket?" I asked gullibly.

"It works," he said, brushing back his dark, windswept hair.

It took me a minute. "Oh, you mean it camouflages you."

"I totally blend into the scenery." This classic grin crept across his face.

I laughed. "Well, I'm glad I know you now," I said truthfully.

Breaking eye contact, I scrambled to my feet and slipped off my chronic Dolce & Gabbana clamdiggers, under which I was wearing the form-fitting Cacharel.

"And I so appreciate your volunteering to help me on this project."

Brandon looked up from his laptop. "Not a hardship," he assured me. He pulled off his schleppy jacket, sort of balled it up, and tossed it onto the sand.

He was wearing a plain black T-shirt with no funny sayings or Nike slogans on it. There was just the choice outline of these excellent cuts flexing through the taut black cotton.

I did this severe *boing!* at the sight of those buff pecs.

Seeing tanned, toned, rock-hard muscles on a male model who highlights his hair is one thing. Discovering them on a gangly poet a stone's throw from geekdom was way different.

"You like the outline?" he asked.

"Seriously slammin'," I said. "I had no idea you were so disciplined with free weights."

The boy looked confused.

"Oh, the outline!" I gasped. "You meant the story outline?" I couldn't believe what I'd blurted. "Oh, I love it. I mean, I think it's a choice tale. It's . . . well, yes, of course, I like it. I've got it right here." I dove back into my bag and rifled through it until my face cooled.

Then I remembered that I'd already taken the outline out. And thrown it at Brandon.

I rolled my eyes and held out my hand, into which the baffled boy placed my clipboard.

We went to work. Brandon was awesome. He was into language the way De and I were into shopping. And just as my big and I could choose the perfect spiky-heeled Manolos to enhance a sleek Michael Kors cashmere, Brandon knew just the right phrase to improve a basic yet blah paragraph.

We were stellar together. I worked with the nouns and

verbs, creating simple, direct sentences as classic and cool as a Calvin Klein pantsuit. "Holding hands, Neve and Jason took the subway to the city," I'd write.

And Brandon would accessorize the sentence with vivid adjectives and totally tasteful modifiers. So in the end, it would go: "Neve, her slim hand shyly clutching Jason's sleeve, sat beside him in the harsh glare of the subway car as the train lurched noisily toward Manhattan."

The boy could shape a paragraph the way Clinique cosmeticians contour an eyebrow. It was towering. Before the sun went down, we'd done a monster makeover on my crew's story.

The first draft was just like Neve Campbell, the real Neve, the way she was in *Party of Five*: Notable, attractive, but just another small-screen, Gen-X ingenue.

Our finished version was the post-*Scream* Neve, all glammed up in a dazzling designer gown and Kevyn Aucoin–quality makeup.

When we got through transforming the tale, it was like, Voilà! An Academy Award presenter is born!

We were so stoked. But also ferociously wiped. "What time is it? My brain is running on empty," I said when we'd read the final paragraph for the fourth time.

Brandon checked his waterproof Casio. It was after four. He shut down his computer. "We did it. It's over. The end," he agreed, flipping down the laptop lid.

I tossed my pen and pink clipboard into the L'Oréal bag, then stood and stretched lazily. "I'll gather my posse, and we can try out the story on them tomorrow."

"Then we'll turn it over to Janet for grammatical tinkering," Brandon said. He grabbed his jacket and got up.

"And then we're done!" I exclaimed.

"You are. I still have to polish *The Tender Tempest*. That's the story I'm doing for Amber," he explained.

"You must really want to meet that guy Shomsky," I said.

"Definitely," Brandon confirmed. "I love his poetry. He's giving a writing workshop this summer that I've already applied for. I probably won't get in. It's fiercely popular and very small, and mostly he takes already published poets."

"You're already published," I said. "I mean, you're the Anonymous who wrote 'Blonde Haze,' aren't you? It was a nimble poem."

"I'm glad you liked it," Brandon said. "It was about you."

"Not even," I went.

He smiled and shrugged. "Well, I didn't actually know you then, so I was free to fantasize. Do you like poetry?"

"Duh, I was like reared on Dr. Suess," I said, but I was still a sentence back, reeling from the revelation that the best poem ever published in the Bronson Alcott *Buzz* was basically based on me.

A couple of serious surfers were riding the tube of a monster wave. We watched them for a while. Then Brandon started to pack up the mats.

"You know, Daddy was once crushed on a poet," I said. "It was when he was in high school. That's where I got the idea for my story."

"Better be careful," Brandon said with this little grin. "It could be genetic."

"Excuse me?" I said cluelessly.

"The crush. The attraction. The pull of the poet," Brandon said. "It could be passed from one generation to another. You never know. It's amazing the kinds of things that run in families."

I laughed. "Do you think that's actually possible?"

"I hope so," he said. He started shaking the sand off the mats. The wind carried a gust of grains my way.

I let out this little yelp and leapt back, covering my face.

"Oh, man, I sandblasted you." Brandon sounded panicked. The next thing I knew, he was prying my hands away from my eyes, going, "Are you okay? Cher, I'm sorry. Did I hurt you? Let me see."

He tilted my chin up and checked me out and started brushing sand off my face. My eyes were squinched shut, but I could feel his fingers softly brushing my cheeks and temples and eyebrows. And then he just stopped.

I opened my eyes narrowly and squinted up into his face.

He was just looking at me. His hands were on my cheeks. He was gently holding my face and looking at me.

Then, abruptly, the buff boy let go of me and stepped back. "You sure you're okay?" he awkwardly asked.

The Ani Niel moment had passed.

"It was way less expensive than a skin peel at Faces," I assured him.

He laughed. "I kept expecting your father to crash through the dunes in full uniform."

"That would be whack," I said, "since Daddy's uniform is a double-breasted Hugo Boss power suit with Gucci loafers."

Brandon shouldered his computer, and we started back to the parking lot.

"The Tender Tempest is an epic title," I said. "So what are we going to call our story?"

He thought about it. *"Unfinished Business?"* he suggested.

"Too corporate," I decided.

"How about . . . *A Time to Remember?"*

"Too Celine Dion." I laughed.

"Could be a song from her *Titanic* period," Brandon cheerfully agreed.

We trudged across the steamy asphalt toward our cars. "What about something simple," I asked as we scooched side by side between our parked vehicles, "like *Jason and Neve: A Love Story?"* I suggested, tossing my bag into my Jeep.

Brandon gave it serious consideration. "Doesn't totally reek," he agreed, dumping his laptop into the front seat of his all-wheel Volvo wagon. "Jason and Neve . . . Neve . . . Never . . . *Never Too Late."*

"Tscha!" I went. "That's it. *Never Too Late."*

"You like that?" he asked, giving me this big grin.

"It rocks the vote." I slapped him an energetic high five. "I think we did it," I said, all stoked. "Brandon, we so cook together!"

"Tell me about it," he murmured as we climbed into our cars.

"Tomorrow," I called.

Chapter 10

So do you want me to order the goodies?" Summer's voice squawked through my speakerphone. "Of the Earth does an awesome brunch platter."

"Not even," De blurted out. She was perched at my dressing table across the room, trying on headbands. I only hoped Summer hadn't heard her.

It was Sunday morning. I was still in my sleep ensemble, boxer shorts and a Hello Kitty T-shirt. Brandon and the rest of my story committee were due in an hour, but my best had come over early.

I rolled my eyes at her grievous lack of tact. "Thanks anyway, Summer," I called toward the speakerphone.

"Okay, well, you never sent back the invite to my parents' recommitment ceremony," she said. "It's next weekend, Cher."

"Omigosh, I can't believe I forgot. I'm sorry, Summer. I've been furiously focused on the contest." I rolled back the mirrored doors of my closet, flipped on the start button, and reviewed the color-coordinated ensembles swishing past on my electronically rotating clothes rack.

"It's scheduled to be the love fest of the century," Summer continued, "a star-studded homage to romance. So then, are you and De planning to attend?"

"Ask her who's catering," De hissed.

"That's trashy. I can't," I whispered back.

"Remember the succotash salsa?" my bud warned.

"Who's catering, Summer?" I tried to sound casual, like it was just this idle question, trifling and insignificant. "I mean, are your parents vegetarians, too?"

De rewarded my bonus question with a thumbs-up sign for creativity.

"I'm ashamed to say they're rabid meat munchers," Summer confessed.

"Tell her I'm in," De whispered.

"Of course, we're coming, Summer," I said, then I silently mouthed to De, Even if we don't have a gift yet. "So we'll see you in a little while."

"You've got filtered water, right?" she wanted to know.

"Bottled Alpine spring," I said, spotting a Kate Moss–style prepster sweater vest spinning on the rack. I flipped the stop switch and took out the pale green vest. Which, I knew at once, would so go with my Daryl K classic low-riding boy-cut pants.

"I better bring my own then," Summer decided. "Catch ya later, girlfriend."

The minute I punched off speaker, De was all, "So you and Word Man ferociously tuned up the tale. That is so dope, girlfriend. What are you going to wear to your romantic rendezvous with Troy?"

With my ensemble over my shoulder, I scuffed toward the bathroom. "I really haven't even thought about that part," I confessed, as much to myself as to my bud. "How whack is that?" I mused.

"Whack squared," De agreed. She was trying on my daisy barrettes, which were the exact replica of the floral hair accessories Drew Barrymore wore at the Oscars. "I mean, isn't sharing a magical moment with the celebrity cover boy the whole point?"

"Well, of course," I said. "I guess I got so caught up in perfecting the story that I forgot why I was doing it. But, De, working with Brandon was so slammin'."

"Also, fun, fabby, frapp, monster, jammin' def, down, and wicked." With this knowing smile, my bud turned from the mirror to face me. "And those are just some of the colorful adjectives you've used to describe the experience. It must have been a ferociously inspiring afternoon."

"He's just good with words," I said.

De raised a skeptical yet shapely eyebrow.

"No, seriously. I mean, how can you compare Brandon to Troy?" I reminded her. "Brandon's just this high school boy who's smart and sensitive and all Ben Affleck–ish and, De, did I mention how pumped he looked in that simple black T-shirt, and that he confided that 'Blonde Haze' was a fantasy about me?"

"While Troy is . . . ?" De prompted.

"Troy? Well, Troy is famous. I mean, everyone knows what's special about him. He's . . . He's like . . . He is so . . ."

"The furious babe?" De helped me along.

"Definitely."

"A hottie of distinction? A tall, emerald-eyed, golden-haired, muscle-oiled, monster model who could have his pick of any Shalom or Tyra?"

"He's the brutal bomb," I assured her. "I've got to shower now. Brandon will be here in five minutes."

"Brandon?" De was laughing at me.

"You know what I mean. Brandon and Murray and Sean and Summer and our entire hard-working, contest-winning crew," I corrected myself. "I can't wait until you guys hear the new and improved story. You're going to be so stoked."

I meant it, too. I could totally imagine my buds grinning with delight as they listened raptly to Brandon's reading.

How wrong was I?

Way.

It was tragic.

I totally hadn't counted on reducing my complete peer group to tears. We were in the den. I'd had the sense to scatter boxes of tissues everywhere. But I couldn't have guessed that we'd go through them in two minutes and grievously start using our name-brand sleeves and shirttails to blot our tears.

First of all, Brandon turned out to be a vicious speaker. Bitterly dramatic. In his rumpled camouflage jacket and wrinkled black jeans, he stood in front of the fireplace and gave this Anthony Hopkins–worthy presentation. It was fully PBS.

And, also, our story had been massively improved. Even though everyone in the room knew what was going to happen, they started getting all misty-eyed around the subway-ride scene and didn't cease blubbering until Jason saw Neve's name in the mirror.

At the end, the den looked like a Kleenex factory after a twister. And my buds were strewn about limp as tissues, too.

It was a triumph.

It was like this triumphant tragedy.

Sean was the first to break the sniffle-filled silence that followed Brandon's reading. Massively moved, he was mashing his Kangol cap in his hands. "Didn't you love that part about Grandma Rose?" he said.

"What part?" Baez asked. Her blue eyeliner was all streaky, and her nose, especially the area around the stud in her nostril, was pitifully enflamed.

"I can't believe you're askin' that." Sean shook his head in disappointment. "It's the *best* part."

"Let me guess," Alana said. "Could it have anything to do with your meager contribution to the tale and like nothing to do with what a brilliant makeover Cher and Brandon did?"

"You're the winner," Sean exalted. "Don't move. Publishers Clearing House has a check for you! I just love that business about the ring and how Jason's old, rich granny gives it to him. That scene was so poignant, you know what I'm saying?"

"No," Summer said.

"That scene," Dionne pointed out, "was about two lines long."

"He's sayin' he loved the two lines he can take credit for," Murray explained.

"Word up. My man understands." Sean gratefully knocked knuckles and elbows with his big.

"Is my feather-light Aveda lash lengthener totally trashed?" De asked. "Is there any left? Do I even care? I am so emotionally dehydrated. You were right, girl-friend. It's a stellar love story."

"Let's hear it for the boy," Murray called, turning to applaud Brandon, who was all busy straightening out the pages he'd read.

Everyone started clapping.

My choice writing partner grinned and dipped his head. Which made his lush dark hair fall forward over his brow again. "It's a good story," he said, flipping back the wayward locks. "I think you guys have a winner here."

"What about you?" Baez asked. "Aren't you in on this?"

"Well, I just worked with your stuff." Brandon got all modest. "It's not really mine."

"You got the gift, haole," Nathan said.

"That was excellent work, man," Murray agreed, pumping Brandon's hand. "Are you available for term papers?"

"He's just kidding," Sean confided. "De does all his term papers."

"You so spruced up that love story, Brandon," De said. "You and Cher work really well together."

"You think so?" The boy was beaming.

"Definitely," Alana declared. "The two of you fashioned a straight-up prize winner."

"Which means," Baez pointed out, "that Cher is going on a dream date for sure!"

"With the world's number one cover babe, Troy!" Summer enthused.

Then the three of them went into their jumping and shrieking act and, simultaneously, started tugging at me.

"Where do you think you'll go on the date?" Alana wanted to know.

"Does it say in the rules?" Baez grilled me. "Oh, what if it's like to Paris or something?"

"Well, I've got to go," Brandon said.

"Really?" I extricated myself from my manic posse and went over to him. "Can't you stay for a little while?" I asked.

"I better not," he said. "I'm going to get a copy of *Never Too Late* over to Janet, so it'll be ready for you by tomorrow. And then I have to finish up *The Tender Tempest*. I'll probably drop it off at Amber's house. And, anyway . . ." He looked over at my hyper homeys. "You've got more important things to do. And I guess I do, too."

"Cher, what are you going to wear?" Summer squealed.

"Who's doing your makeup?" Alana demanded.

"Let's go upstairs and look through your closet," Baez begged.

"Uh-oh," Sean looked at Murray. "It's getting all girly around here."

"Come on, Sean." Alana grabbed the boy's arm. "Help us. You know what boys like."

"Did I hear my beeper going off?" Murray said with bogus urgency.

"Time to make the doughnuts," Nathan agreed, getting ready to go.

"Stay," De commanded.

"On the other hand," Murray mused aloud, "the game's on in five minutes, and we got chips, dip, and a monster TV right here."

"Solid plan," Nathan agreed. "We stay."

"Good boys," De said distractedly. She wasn't actually paying that much attention to them. Her classic hazel eyes were busy sizing up Brandon and me, and shining with this mischievous gleam.

I walked Brandon to the door.

"Sorry you've got to rush off," I said. "Thanks again for all your help."

He gave me his easy grin. "Anytime," he said softly.

I watched him walk to his car. He didn't look back. He didn't wave. He was on his way to Amber's house, and he couldn't care less about celebrating our collaboration.

Suddenly this heinous thought crossed my mind. It went, like, maybe he doesn't like me.

But then, a lifetime of experience said, As if! and wiped that icky thought away.

I sighed, turned to go back into the house, and almost bumped into De. "He lied," she said, barely able to stifle her glee.

"Brandon?"

"Trust me," De urged, smiling full out now. "When he said he had more important things to do? Hel-*lo,* fib, falsehood, prevarication, bogus sham," she said. "Girlfriend, there is nothing more urgent on that boy's agenda than you. You could see it all over his not too shabby face. Cher, the bard of Bronson Alcott is fully crushed on you."

"Not even," I protested, but the heaviness I'd tried to sigh away lifted just a little. "De, he ducked out of here the first chance he got. And at the beach, when he was inches from me and had a clean shot at a sandy kiss, he took a total pass and started talking about Daddy."

"I don't know about the seaside smooch," De admitted as we headed back to the den, "but his recent retreat was all about your upcoming rendezvous with Troy."

"You think?" I had to consider my bud's point of view. De is wise in the ways of love. With a snap of her julietted fingertips, the girl makes Murray sit, heel, or beg.

"Well, if the boy's all bent over that, it's way premature," I said. "My date with Troy is so not a certainty. Though I have to say, I can't imagine Ani Niel finding a more romantic story."

Our English class so agreed.

"Before we begin the reading," I announced to them on Monday morning, "my buds will be passing out tissues among you."

"Is your tale that pitiful? Why am I not surprised?" Amber sniped.

"No, it's just extremely moving," Summer told her.

"This story is rated MTJ," Sean said. "Major tear-jerker."

I missed the rest of my peers' warm-up routine because just then Brandon came over with Janet's spell-checked, gramatically correct version of our story.

"Well, good luck," the tall boy said, pressing the paper into my hand and holding my hand with both of his. "I hope you win, Cher, if that's what you want."

"If I do win, it'll be because of you," I said.

"Don't remind me," he said, with a smile more bittersweet than a dark chocolate Dove bar. "That Troy's a lucky guy."

"Cher, let's get going," Mr. Stanky called.

Before I could say anything else, Brandon let go of my hand and headed back to his desk.

The class was clamoring for me. I smiled. I waved. I

went, "Okay, people. Our story is called *Never Too Late.*"

"Mad cool title!" "Awesome!" kids shouted. "It sounds so real." "You go, girl." "Is that little pink tee Mossimo? I saw that exact velvet mini at Fred Hayman Beverly Hills." "Cher rules!"

I cleared my throat and waited for the comments and applause to stop. Then I began to read our tale. " 'Jason had no idea the girl was a poet. He'd never noticed her before. Was it possible that this raven-haired young beauty had been in his class for months?' "

I kept reading, but those first three sentences so stayed with me. How could I not have seen the similarity before?

I felt like the stooge supreme. A blind Moe. Switch the sexes, make it now, and it wasn't just Daddy's frantically romantic love story that Brandon and I had worked on. It could have been our own.

If, of course, we were high school sweethearts crushed on each other. Which, I guessed, we weren't.

I mean, hadn't I gotten involved in this entire situation because of Troy?

If I hadn't met the monster babe at the mall, I wouldn't have snagged a copy of Ani's book.

Without the book, I wouldn't have gotten caught reading a romance novel during class time.

If I hadn't been busted with Ani's book, Mr. Stanky wouldn't have known anything about the contest or decided to enroll my entire class in the project.

And then I'd probably never have gotten to know Brandon or work so closely with him or have such a fun afternoon at Malibu, even if he didn't kiss me.

None of that would have happened without Troy.

Still, the similarity between Daddy and Ina, and Brandon and me was kind of interesting. Kind of, actually, like Brandon's joke about poet-worship being passed from one generation to another.

I just kept reading. A sniffle from the audience caught my attention. I looked up and saw that the class tear-fest had begun.

By the time I finished, Mr. Stanky had sent a sobbing Tiffany Gelfin to the school nurse, and Sharon, the grunge queen, got an EMS ride to Cedars-Sinai. She'd gotten seriously caught up in the story and accidentally pulled the safety pin out of her eyebrow.

Still, Stanky was pysched. "Well, class, I think our story is ready to send off to the contest. I'm going to pop it into the mailbox myself."

"Mailbox!" everyone started raving.

"You're sending it regular snail mail?" De objected. "Since when was Beverly Hills declared a FedEx-free zone?"

"Overnight it," Sean insisted.

"Same day it," Murray said.

Amber stood, which wasn't easy since she was encased in this puckered, size-two, strapless tube dress that cleverly simulated full-body cellulite.

"My contest entry is called *The Tender Tempest*," she announced, waiting until the round of admiring comments and a smattering of applause died down. "And my assistant, Sari Stickland, is going to hand-deliver it to Ani K. Niel's Holmby Hills mansion today! Right after she proofs it, fills out the entry form, and picks up the vintage Chanel I'm having altered on Melrose."

"Mr. Stanky! Mr. Stanky!" Summer popped up. "I've got to run an errand for my parents in the elegant

Holmby area," she said. "I can drop *Never Too Late* at Ani's door—right after my shiatsu massage."

"Class?" Mr. Stanky called for consensus. "Is that agreeable?"

And twenty-three out of our remaining twenty-four classmates went, "Way!"

Chapter 11

*T*he very next day, after school, I arrived home to a major surprise.

I threw my petite Prada purse onto my bed and went to feed Ben. Then I raced to my cellular and speed-dialed my true blue.

"Hang on to your classic crocheted hat, girlfriend," I commanded. "You are so not going to believe this."

"If it pertains to the Easter Bunny or Santa Claus, you're probably wrong," De said. "I'm a fierce fan of both."

"I think that Ben is a Betty!" I practically shouted.

"Ben, who Tiffany Fukashima fixed up with Baez that Halloween when Amber wore the tight white sheath she snagged from the sales rack at Neiman's and Ryder thought she came as a mummy so she won first prize but heinously trashed the party?"

"Duh. Not that Ben," I said.

"Tell me you're not talking about Ben the babe from the Academy Award–winning team of Matt the hottie and Ben the babe?"

"Ben Affleck? Why would I call him a Betty?" I asked.

"Can we skip the Q and A and get to the breaking news segment?" De urged. "I'm on the other line with Murray."

"Ben the fish!" I said. "Our fish. Ben just had babies. Like a gazillion of them."

"Our little baby Ben? Does that mean our mall hop is canceled?" De asked. "I mean, do you feel like you have to stay home and be supportive—or whatever?"

"Oh, wow. I totally forgot. We were going to look for Summer's parents' gift."

"Hang on for a second," De said. "I want to tell Murray I'm a grandmother."

Cell phone to my ear, I hurried downstairs to find a bigger bowl for Ben. Another call came in while I was in the pantry, searching through the crystal and china. There was this monster lucite salad bowl that looked like a possibility.

"Hello, is Cher Horowitz there?" a woman's voice asked.

"She is. She's me," I went. "Who's this?"

"This is Devora Mott, Ani Niel's assistant," she said.

"Quit it, De!" I went. "I'm trying to find a props bowl for the babies."

There was a silence.

And in that silence, I thought, why would my big tease me about the contest now?

And then I thought, she wouldn't.

Which was when it occurred to me that the Moe making the call didn't sound anything like De.

So finally, I said, "Who is this? I mean, who is this really?"

And the woman went, "Hold on a moment, please." Which I did.

And then another voice came on and went, "Cher, this is Ani Niel. Are you the Cher Horowitz who attends Bronson Alcott High School in Beverly Hills?"

"Uh-huh" was all I could manage.

"Whose name was listed as one of the authors of a story called *Never Too Late?*"

"Uh-huh," I repeated.

"Your story was very interesting. Very," Ani said.

"Uh-huh," I went again, starting to sound like the guy in *Sling Blade.*

"Cher, I wonder if you could stop by Heartland, my estate. I'd like to meet you. I'd like to talk with you about your contest entry," she said.

"Really?" I said, wandering out of the pantry into the kitchen.

"I'm going to put Devora back on. I hope she can set something up with you," Ani said. "I think you and your classmates sent in a wonderful contest entry."

"Thank you." It was like my tongue had been short-sheeted.

The minute Devora got back on the line, my call waiting clicked. I grabbed a pencil and scrawled down Ani's Holmby Hills address and her assistant's instructions, and finally I said that there was someone on the other line and hit call waiting.

"De?" I hollered.

"Murray thinks we should call him Mrs. Doubtfire because of the gender confusion," my bud said.

"De, we're over Ben," I blurted. "Ani Niel just called me!"

"Not even!" she shrieked.

"Even," I insisted. "She read our contest entry, and she wants me to come see her."

"Be still, my heart!" De said, all stoked. "Does that mean we won?"

I hadn't had time to psych it out. "What do you think?" I asked, volleying the ball back into De's court.

"Why else would she want to see you?" my bud queried. "Duh, yes. I think that's what it means."

"But Summer just delivered our story yesterday. I don't even think the deadline for entries has passed," I reasoned.

De wasn't listening. "Hang on," she hollered. "I want to tell Murray we won!"

"De, wait," I shouted, but I was talking to dead air. A second later call-waiting clicked again. I hit the button. It was Summer.

"Wait'll you hear. Wait'll you hear!" she hyperventilated.

"Summer, where were you today?" I asked our bud, who had been absent from school.

"Everywhere!" The girl moaned. "I had to run a million errands for my mom. She's been in treatment for perfectionism, and putting on this love fest has thrown her into a brutal relapse. I hope the marriage lasts through the celebration. So anyway, I promised to share her chores. Which is why I'm calling you—"

"Summer," I interrupted, "I've got De on the other line. Plus this amazing thing just happened—"

She kept on talking. "Guess who's going to read at my parents' gala?"

And I was all, "Guess who called me five minutes ago?"

And then we both went, "Ani K. Niel! Aaaaah!"

De clicked in again. When I told her Summer was on the other line, she suggested a four-way conference call. I relayed the plan to Summer on my way back upstairs, hung up, and waited until the pink console phone in my room rang. Then, when the four of us were hooked up, I said, "Okay, who goes first?"

Summer called it. "So yesterday after school, I had to hand-deliver these invitations to certain celebs who are coming to my parents' love fiesta," she breathlessly related. "I didn't know who was on the list when I agreed to drop our story at Ani's. I just knew that one of the stars lived in Holmby Hills. And it turned out to be Ani!"

"What does she look like?" De asked.

"Her assistant answered the door," Summer confided.

"Devora?" I said.

Summer squealed with delight. "How'd you know?!"

"Yeah," Murray said. "How did you?"

I clued them in on the contents of my call and then Murray said, "So who's going with you?"

"Excuse me? Who's going with me where?" I asked.

"To Ani's," De chimed in. "Murray's right, Cher. Even though you and Brandon polished the gem, lots of people mined the raw material."

"I'm in," Summer shouted. "What time are we going?"

So it was, as they say in story speak, that a committee of my peers was selected the next day in Mr. Stanky's class to join me at Ani Niel's sprawling chateau, Heartland.

From its gated, gold-leafed entrance to the heart-shaped hedges lining the drive, to the great lawn strewn with Cupid statuary and fountains, to the soaring, gilded, stadium-size structure that was the main house, Heartland was bitterly chronic.

Ani had sent her limousine for me. When the classic stretch stopped at the columned entrance to Heartland, Murray, Sean, Summer, De, Brandon, and I piled out, awestruck despite our many personal encounters with flashy opulence.

The place was a monster showcase.

A couple of vans were parked at the side of the house, I noticed. Thick cables snaked from one of the trucks and disappeared through a lush thicket of pink peonies and roses. They looked like TV vans. I wondered if Ani was in the middle of a Barbara Walters moment. Of course, it could have been just Diane, Katie, Jane, or even *Extra*.

As I and my buds scrambled out of the mile-long white stretch limo that the celebrity author had sent for us, a smaller black limousine with tinted windows came crunching up the pebbled driveway.

De squinted at the shiny vehicle. "I know that Mercedes hearse," she said, annoyed.

"It's Amber," Summer gasped.

"Could the contest have ended in a tie?" I wondered aloud.

The limo with the vanity plate RICH MD pulled up just behind us. But at that moment, Ani's butler opened the colossal front door to her casa and we all spun toward it.

A plump, pretty woman, in a cable knit cashmere dress that looked way Tse, rushed out of the house to greet us. I just knew she was Devora. Her brow wrinkled briefly at the sight of my crew.

I mean, we definitely looked dope. We were decked out in our neon-bright name-brand ensembles, all youthful, energetic, and scrubbed. I was in this cute little lime shirt with hot pink piping and these fine floral capri leggings from Victoria Secret's Romantic Dreams and Fantasies catalog. But Devora was obviously surprised to see so many of us.

But the woman was a solid professional. She got over it fast. "I'm Devora Mott. Welcome to Heartland," she called from the veranda.

At that moment, Amber alighted from her cramped limo. Which was bad enough. But suddenly, Sari slithered out behind her.

"Double trouble," Sean said.

They were in these identical long-sleeved faux lizard spandex bodysuits that made them look like mother and daughter space invaders from the planet Snake.

"Cher?" Devora called pleasantly. "Which one of you is Cher Horowitz?"

"I am," I answered, smiling and waggling my fingers at her. "I'm the one you spoke with on the phone, Devora."

"And I'm Amber Marins," Amber said, breezing right by me to shake Devora's hand.

My mouth fell open.

"Fly-catcher," Sari snickered, following Amber.

A cloud of confusion crossed Devora's basically competent face as she shook Amber's paw. "I'm sorry," she said softly. "I don't think I know you."

"Amber Marins, Dr. Marins's comely and talented little girl and the author of *The Tender Tempest*," Amber announced. "And these are my fans."

A dangerous growl escaped De's throat, but Murray grabbed her arm and restrained her from lunging at the Doublemint dorks on the veranda.

I hurried to Devora, hoping to rescue Ani's distressed assistant. "Hi, I'm Cher," I said again. "This place is so def, and I so admire Ani's work so I'm like so stoked that you invited me."

"So, so, so what?" Sari snarled.

Devora put her arm around me and drew me aside. "Who are all these other people?" she asked softly.

"Well, the buff team down there are some of my buds who worked long and hard on *Never Too Late*. Our class felt that they would represent our best and brightest."

"And the girls in green?" she asked.

"Didn't you invite them?" I said.

Devora shook her head. "I don't think so," she said. "But I'll check with Ani. She's very eager to see you."

"And we're like brutally stoked about meeting her," I acknowledged.

"Actually, Cher. I think she'd like to talk with you privately," Devora confided.

I glanced at my buds. Devora picked up on my dilemma at once.

"Your friends can wait for you out on the terrace. There's a buffet set up near the pool. It'll be fun for them," she promised.

"I think they'd rather meet Ani," I mused.

"The cover of Ani's new book is being photographed down at the pool. And one of the networks is doing a piece about the making of a romance book cover," she said, pointing toward the vans parked at the far corner of the casa. "They're taping it today. If your friends are quiet, I don't think anyone will mind them watching."

"A cover shoot?" Amber's sonar kicked in.

"Yes," Devora said, taking the lizard sisters by the arm. "Would everyone like to meet Alison Banks, the popular young soap star?" She was addressing my homeys now.

"Alison Banks! Where? Where?" Sean started quivering like a hunting dog on point.

"She makes Tiffani-Amber Thiessen look like Tori Spelling," Murray noted.

De shot him a warning glare. "Heel," she ordered.

"What'd I do?" Murray got all defensive.

"You're drooling," De pointed out.

"And"—Devora finished her sales pitch—"Ani's most famous model, Troy."

"Where do I sign?" De said.

"Troy is here?" Summer looked ready to lift off. I was sure she was going to grab Brandon's arms and start doing her pogo-stick jump. "Isn't that chronic?" she asked the boy.

Brandon shrugged. He was the only member of my team who didn't seem thrilled with the news. He glanced up at me, gave me this supportive smile, then looked away.

"All right, everyone, come with me," Devora said, leading Amber and Sari around the side of the house. "I'm going to get you all settled. Cher, why don't you go right inside. Ask Tom to see you to the blue room. I'll be back in a minute."

De rushed over and gave me a hug. "Good luck, girlfriend," she whispered, then hurried after our buds.

Chapter 12

I watched my crew disappear around the corner of the house, then went inside. Ani's butler, Tom, was waiting for me.

I trailed him up a flight of stairs as wide as a freeway. On every landing, there were marble statues of cupids carrying humongous pitchers in addition to their bows and arrows. And the pitchers were overflowing with massive fresh flower arrangements.

After padding down a plushly carpeted hallway, Tom knocked softly on a door. "Miss Cher is here," he called, then turning to me, he said, "You're expected. Go right in, please."

From the grandeur of the house and grounds and all the hearts and cupids, I expected to be greeted by a white-haired prima donna in a flowing pastel evening gown draped over a chaise longue, dictating her next book to a secretary.

Duh, I was so wrong.

Ani wasn't young exactly. I mean, she had to be about Daddy's age, but she was a frantic babe. Curvaceously slender, she was sleekly garbed in Donna Karan, the same black trousers and gauzy coatdress that I'd tabbed with a yellow stickie in the spring issue of *Elle*. Her thick black hair was casually roped into a single braid. And her smile was stellar.

"Cher," she said. "I've so looked forward to meeting you."

"Me, too," I went, taking the hand she extended. "I just started reading your books, and I'm thinking of opening a charge account at Rexall Square just to cover my tissue expenses."

Ani laughed this easy tinkly laugh. "Well, I enjoyed reading your story, too," she said.

The room was piled with books. They were stacked everywhere, not just on shelves, but on chairs, tables, the floor, and Ani's huge mahogany desk, which all by itself was as big and messy as De's little brother's room. There were award plaques from the Romance Writers of America and other organizations on the wall behind Ani's desk and framed letters from famous people. I even saw one from Harold Shomsky, Brandon's favorite poet.

"Do you know him personally?" I asked. "I have a friend who's a big fan of his."

Ani said she did. Then she asked me to sit down. And we sat on these little apricot velvet sofas, facing each other across this low table that was all antiquely nicked up. The manila envelope from our school was sitting smack in the center of that table.

Ani tapped it. "Where did you get the idea for this story?" she asked.

"Well, first of all, I didn't write it alone," I started to explain.

"I know," Ani said. "It arrived with the note from your teacher saying that it was a class project. But did you come up with the plot?"

"Sort of," I confessed. And then I told her about how Daddy had come into my room to comfort me and we'd had this Oprah Book Club moment, where he'd suddenly shared his deeply moving story of young love with me, which I and my posse then accessorized and updated.

"So in a way, it's your fault," I concluded, "because if I hadn't been brutally torn up over *What the Heart Remembers,* Daddy would never have told me his tale of teen angst."

"How is he?" Ani asked softly.

"Daddy? He's excellent," I told her. "I have him on a low-fat, low-cholesterol, low-salt, sugar-free diet, and while he gets a little snappish sometimes, he's bitterly healthy and lookin' totally fresh."

Ani nodded and gave me this starry-eyed smile. It reminded me of the way Daddy looked at me the night he unloaded his Ina saga.

She got up and walked over to the French windows, which looked out at the rambling grounds three stories below.

"Your friends seem to be enjoying themselves," she said.

I went over to the window and stood beside her.

The area around the pool was lit up brighter than sunlight by these big lamps with silver reflecting umbrellas attached to them. There were cables taped everywhere. People scurried around, stepping over them, carrying costumes, and setting up cameras and sound equipment, and putting pond lilies and reeds, which I guessed were plastic but looked excellently real, into the shallow end of the pool. Only the stars were at rest, sort of.

Alison Banks was on the porch of one of the poolside cabanas. She was being videotaped having her hair done. The young soap diva was decked out in your basic damsel dress, a pinched-waist purple confection with yards of satiny skirt. The girl was a brutal dish.

Sean and Murray were hovering beside her hairdresser, holding trays of brushes, spritz cans, and other coiffure equipment, and grinning furiously into the camera.

Brandon was standing near the catering table where a lavish feast was spread. The boy poet was talking to a guy in jeans who was wearing a wireless headset and toting your basic techy clipboard.

Surrounded by my girl buds, Troy was sitting in one of the folding chairs beside the pool. Even with this makeup bib draped over the front of his flowing cavalier's shirt, you knew how brutally washboard his abs were. And his long golden locks glinted gorgeously under the spotlights. Ivan had done a killer job on his hair.

I couldn't believe I was going to spend a romantic evening with the studly star. "Ani," I said, "I'm seriously stoked that you chose our story, especially since the deadline for entries is still a couple of weeks away. What clinched it for you?"

"Excuse me?" she said. Then something clicked and she went, "Oh, my gosh. I'm sorry, Cher. I didn't mean to mislead you. Your story hasn't won. My staff has just started reading the entries. There are thousands of them."

I felt like such a bonehead. I looked out the window again and saw my frolicking buds three stories below enjoying their moment of innocence, still believing that we were winners. Which, of course, in all the ways that count, we were.

It was just this passing icky feeling. My basic nature is all upbeat. I'm a total cork on the waters of life. I can be buffeted by the waves of ill fortune, but I'm unsinkably optimistic. I so ferociously float.

"Then why did you call me? Why did you want to speak to me?" I asked, seeing not just my clueless crew plus Amber and Sari, but Troy, too, who now seemed so near yet so far away. "And how come you personally read our entry?"

"It must have been fate," Ani said. I glanced at her and saw that she was smiling. She looked much kinder than the bummer she'd just delivered. "I was just rifling through the entries. And what first interested me was that yours was the only one from a school, an entire class. Then I saw your name listed as one of the editors, which piqued my curiosity."

"Oh, you mean *Cher*. My best bud, Dionne, and I were named for pop idols of our parents' generation," I explained.

"No, I mean Horowitz," Ani said. "I once knew a boy named Melvin Horowitz—"

"Get out," I went. "That's Daddy's name. But his friends all call him Mel."

"Somehow I knew that," Ani said, mysteriously, with that same warm smile. "So I read your story. And I got terribly curious about it. About many things, like . . .

the business about Neve deciding to reverse her name? Who came up with that idea?"

"You mean Jason's name," I reminded her. "Neve didn't use her own name to sign her work, she used his, backward. You know, like Jason. Nosaj."

"But, you see, what's so remarkable, Cher, is that that is almost exactly what I did. Except that I used my own name in reverse."

"Not even!" I said, thinking, Tscha! what a coincidence! "So, you mean, Ani's not your real name. It's . . ." It took me a second. "It's Ina?"

"Like Neve, I reversed the last name, as well," she said.

I was trying to picture her whole name backward when Ani or Ina or whoever she was said, "Ani K. Niel. That's Ina K-lein, Cher. My real name is Ina Klein."

"Ina Klein?" I was stunned. "Daddy's Ina?" My mouth flopped open, and for a minute I couldn't speak. I must've looked like Ben at feeding time, I thought. And then I remembered that Ben wasn't really a Ben!

"I'm suffering this harsh reality crisis," I blurted. "I feel all Gillian Anderson. This is way beyond coincidental. It's full-out *X-Files*. Plus now I don't even know what to call you!"

"Call me Ani," she said. "I'm used to it now. And, Cher, I'm having a little reality crisis myself. I need to ask a very big favor of you? I'd like this to be our secret for now."

"Excuse me," I said, pressing the pause button. "I think Daddy should know."

"I promise you he will," Ani said. "It's been a very long time, Cher. I'm not sure how he'll feel about it or, for that matter, how I will, after all these years. I don't want to do it by telephone or mail. I just need a little time."

"But I have to tell De," I protested. "She's my true blue best friend. I tell her everything."

"Just for a little while," Ani urged.

I had another thought. "Does this mean we might still win the contest? I mean, our story is not just a five-thousand-word crying jag. It's like so real life, right?"

She took my arm. "I'm afraid it probably means just the opposite, Cher. The fact that your father and I are old friends, however coincidental or *X-Files* that may be, would make it seem like favoritism, like something not quite fair about your entry winning."

"But it isn't just my entry," I reminded her. "Our entire class worked on it. And Mr. Stanky, our English teacher, is frantic to bring the cash and prizes home to Bronson Alcott. Other than the dream date, of course, which my fans insisted be my particular reward for a job well done. Plus, everyone, except a certain redheaded competitor, thinks Troy and I are awesome dating material."

"Would you like to meet him now?" Ani suggested.

"Hello, I've already met the babe. My buds and I ran into him at the mall when he was autographing *What the Heart Remembers*. He totally owes his exceptional new hair coloring to my man Ivan at Rocket."

There was a knock at the door. "Ani," Devora called, "they're ready for you downstairs."

"I need a few more minutes," Daddy's former flame answered. She turned to me. "Cher, will you give me a day to think over what we've talked about? Just twenty-four hours?"

I hate to keep things from Daddy. I only do it when it's essential to his health and welfare. Like if I get a B or a C on some pop quiz and haven't had time to discuss the matter with the teacher in question. I mean, like why stress Daddy out? After I've negotiated the grade up to an A, I totally fill him in.

Daddy is way proud of my bargaining ability. He always says that if I had a vicious streak I'd make a chronic lawyer.

I guessed I could hide the truth from him for just one day.

But, whew, I thought. It would be agony keeping a secret so buff from De. Still, I agreed to do it.

"Just for the record," I added as Ani walked me to her office door, "Daddy's not dating anyone at the moment."

"Well, there's another coincidence," the author said brightly. "Neither am I."

Ani told her assistant that she'd be down in a little while. I left her there and followed Devora downstairs.

The moment we set foot on the slate terrace, Amber, in her little green pod suit, rushed up to us. "Could you have taken any longer monopolizing Ms. Niel's valuable time?" she asked loudly, practically knocking me over to get to Devora.

"Amber, right?" Ani's assistant said. "You're a friend of Cher's."

"Does Ani like Cher?" Amber asked.

Devora nodded. "I believe she does."

"Cher and I are very close," Amber said, sliding her arm through mine and giving Devora a smile as bright and bogus as her hair color. "We've known each other for years. Ah, but why dwell on Cher's good fortune. Mine is that I'm blessed with so more than mere beauty. I'm a talented writer. I do poetry, songs, stories, pep squad cheers. And if my old friend Cher didn't chat Ani into a coma, I'd appreciate my own private moment with the queen of romance."

"She'll be down in a little while," Devora assured her.

Amber released me and stared at the woman. "While those Paloma Picasso earrings you're wearing are easy on the eye, Devora, they may be impairing your hearing. I think I said *private.*"

"Amber, what are you doing here, anyway?" I asked.

"I'm in Mr. Stanky's class, too," she snapped. Then she looked back at Devora and smiled again. "And I'm here to support my peers."

There was a sudden commotion. Devora looked past us. I turned to see what was happening and was temporarily blinded by a barrage of flashbulbs going off.

It was Troy. Striding toward us, in his flowing white cavalier's shirt, buckskin tights, and thigh-high boots, he looked every flexed inch the studly swashbuckler. Two photographers were running beside him, snapping pictures, while a TV crew scampered behind them, taping the cover boy's every move.

As my eyesight cleared, I noticed my crew waving from the catering table where they were enjoying a gourmet gorge. I felt a grueling tug of guilt at the sight of De. I so longed to share every moment of my Ani encounter with her, but that would have to wait.

Brandon was standing beside my best bud. He threw me this excellent smile.

"I think you've already met Amber," Devora was saying to Troy as I waved to Brandon. "And this is Cher Horowitz."

Suddenly, Troy swept me off my feet. Literally. He picked me up and spun me toward the cameras. "Fellas, this is Cher," he announced. "She's someone you ought to interview. She's a big fan of mine."

"And what am I, chopped liver?" A shrill voice that wasn't Amber's rang out.

Everyone turned. "I may be only a ninth grader," Sari shouted, worming her way through the crowd, "but nobody gets to diss Dr. Strickland's little girl."

Amber gasped. "Sari," she shouted. "Your father is not a doctor."

"And that's not your first nose," her protégé snapped. "Don't get your body suit in a twist, Red. It's just an expression. Troy, I'm a major admirer," she told the boy, who was cradling me in his arms. "Every cover you've ever been on is tacked up on my wall. I've memorized your vital stats, know your birthplace, siblings' names and ages, and your parents' occupations. I've even got your name tatooed on my bicep!"

Troy dropped me as suddenly as he'd swept me up.

The cameras, too, turned toward Sari as the frizzy-haired girl rolled up her spandex sleeve and displayed her tattoo. There on her slender bicep, Troy's name was scripted in gothic letters and tucked inside a ballpoint-inked red heart.

"You didn't have that tattoo at lunchtime," Amber accused.

"You didn't have that nose at birth," Sari responded as the cameras focused in on her arm graffiti. "That's Sari with an *i*," she told an interviewer scribbling notes.

My perky lime blouse was all schmeared with body makeup, I noticed. And there were oil patches on the back of my leggings where Troy's arms had cradled me.

"Now, here's the little gal you guys should interview," he was saying, beaming at Sari. "She's my number one fan."

Amber looked stunned. I put my arm around her. "I'm sure she didn't mean it," I said as the journalists and TV crew followed Sari and Troy back to the pool.

"And I'm sure you don't mean to live your life as a happy Keebler elf, Alice in Wonderland, or a walking smiley face." Amber pulled away from me. "Don't ever lose that sweet innocence, Cher," she said. "I taught that kid everything she knows. Do you have any idea how proud I am?"

As Amber rushed off after Sari, Troy, and the cameras, De and my pals came running over.

"What's Ani like?" Summer wanted to know. "She wasn't wearing fur, was she?"

"Yo, break it down. Did she say we're the winners?" Murray asked.

"Did you tell her how I came up with the Grandma Rose angle?" Sean queried.

De squeezed my hands. "Dish, girlfriend. I can't wait to hear what happened."

"And I can't wait to tell you, De, but I have to," I said anxiously.

"Excuse me?" My bud tried to take a step back, but I held on to her hands. "Are you saying that there's something you can't share with me?"

"No, not exactly," I said. "I'm just asking you to delay dish gratification for one day. Dionne," I implored, "this news is so sizzling it'll still be hot tomorrow. Trust me, girlfriend. Pretty, pretty please." I looked around. "Hey, where's Brandon?" I asked.

"He took off," Summer replied. "Like when Troy

picked you up. One minute Brandon was standing between De and me, all smiling and waving, and then he was gone. Right, De?"

"Right," my best friend said. "He left . . . just like this." And she turned on her kiwi-colored Diego Della Valle driving shoes and stalked away.

Chapter 13

Normally, I don't do despair. My life is too fun and full of friends. So many people love and need me that I'm always busy giving of myself. Yet in my sumptuous room that evening, the bitter taste of solitude washed down the slice of pizza I'd grabbed on the way home from Ani's.

Icky things were piling up.

Brandon and De had walked out on me. The rest of my gang was ticked off because all I could tell them was that no, we hadn't won the contest. We'd been sort of disqualified. But I couldn't explain why because that would have meant ratting out Ani's secret.

To make matters worse, Summer's parents' party was only days away, and I'd gotten so sidetracked with story writing that De and I had never gone back to the mall to pick up the memory album for the Finkel-Dworkins.

Plus, even Daddy had forsaken me. He was out for the

evening at a black-tie business dinner. Earlier in the day, I'd picked out the Zegna tux he was going to wear and hung it on the oak valet in his dressing room along with a buff linen shirt, formal socks, and a tie.

I would have felt utterly alone, except that my room was teeming with fish. Ben's teeny golden babies were my only company that evening. They were so adorable, all five hundred or so of them.

Our humongous lucite salad bowl looked like rush hour on the Santa Monica freeway. And that was after I'd scooped babies into every available cup and bowl in the house. I knew I couldn't keep all my little goldies. They deserved better accommodations. Plus, sooner or later, Daddy would want a sip of water and it would be like, whoops, no glass!

Suddenly, I had this inspired gift idea. Before I knew what I was doing, I had dialed De's number.

"Hi, this Dionne," her machine answered. "I can't come to the phone right now. Either that, or I'm screening my calls. Press one if you want to leave a pager number. Press two to leave a voice message. And if your name happens to be Cher Horowitz, please hang up. I'm so not interested."

"Dionne, it's me," I said, after the long annoying series of beeps. "I've got a dynamite idea for Goldie and Chuck's recommitment bash. Please pick up. Well, at least, call me back, okay?" I urged, then hung up.

Here I was with this awesome idea that I needed De to help make come true. The long arm of lonesomeness seized me again. I threw myself back on my classic pink chaise longue and stared at the ceiling—which, actually, has this pretty pale blue skyscape of clouds and stars painted on it.

About a minute later, I jumped up. While it may feel

yucky at the beginning, solitude can so stoke the creative juices. Suddenly, I was like this furious idea factory. It was so Martha Stewart.

I phoned Summer. She picked up on the second ring. "Hey, Sum," I said. "It's Cher."

"Big deal." She sounded frosted.

"Summer, you can't be mad at me. I told you Ani wasn't wearing fur. In fact, she seems like the kind of person who'd set up a sanctuary for abandoned shellfish. Anyway," I moved on, "you said that she's coming to your parents' party, didn't you?"

"De's here, and you're on speakerphone," Summer said, which so explained the chilly reception.

"De," I called. "Girlfriend, I just left a message on your machine."

There was a moment of silence. Then Summer went, "She just handed me a note. It says, 'Tell Cher I'm not speaking to her.'"

"What's De doing there anyway?" I asked. "It's late."

"She's sleeping over. We're like having a pajama party, I guess," Summer reported. "Whoops, hold on. I'm getting another note."

"De, this is silly," I called. "We can speak. We can reason together. We've been best buds since grade school."

"Okay, here it is." Summer was back. " 'Tell Cher that we're bonding.' Okay, Cher? So that's what De's doing at my house. Actually, I was wondering. And, yes, Ani's on the guest list. She's going to do one of the toasts. She's my mom's favorite author. Goldie ran into her at the Nature Oasis spa. Well, technically, Ani ran into Goldie. Mom was getting her legs waxed, and she was screaming so loudly that the woman being massaged in the next booth came charging in draped in one of those

130

pink terry towels and it was Ani. Mom says she was so supportive."

"Supportive, not secretive," I heard De's voice in the background.

"Dionne, you'll fully understand tomorrow," I said. "Ani's got this righteous dilemma to work out, and in fact, I'm trying to help her solve it now so that I can spill everything to you at the earliest possible moment."

Silence. Then, "Er, Cher," Summer said.

"Just read it," I went.

"Okay, De says, 'Tell her that if she salami promises . . .'"

"Solemnly promises," De grumbled in the distance.

"Well, excuse me, Dionne," Summer snapped back, "but your handwriting is worse than my dad's nutritionist's. I mean, my dad was sucking seaweed for a month before we realized the guy had written soy beans."

"Summer," I said, "please continue."

"Okay, but it's really hard to read," she carped. "So I guess it's if you solemnly promise that she'll be the first person you tell all to, that she'll call a twenty-four-hour amnesia on this feud."

"Amnesty," De hollered. "Amnesty means a pardon, a forgiveness of grievances. Amnesia is like brain damage, Summer."

"Oh, big deal. Why don't you tell her yourself?" Summer retorted.

"I accept!" I shouted. "Dionne, you are definitely my first off ramp on the hot gossip highway. So, Summer, is there a chance Goldie and Chuck could squeeze in one more guest at their love fest?"

"I'm dying. Dying!" Summer shrieked. "You're bringing Troy!"

"Not even," I said. "The rude boy so dumped me. What would I want with that random hunk?"

"You're coming with Brandon, aren't you?" It was De.

"I wish," I found myself saying. Then I sighed. "Dionne, hel-*lo*. He walked out on me."

"Doubly dumped," Summer said. "Whew, loser day for you, right?"

"Forgive her, Cher," De said. "Our bud has a blurting disorder."

"I want to bring Daddy," I told them.

"Oh, that's so sweet," Summer cooed. "Like when I had zits in fifth grade and no one would ask me to the dance so my dad took me and, well, actually, it was extremely embarrassing."

"Let it pass," De urged me.

"So is that a yes?" I asked Summer. "Is it okay for Daddy to come?"

"Let's see, we've sent out five hundred invites. And gotten back five hundred and forty-two Will Attends. What's another gate crasher, more or less? If he's appropriately dressed, Mel is like totally welcome. I'll put him on the list."

"Thanks, Summer," I said. "Oh, and I've got the cleanest gift idea. De, do your parents still have those heartshaped little glass candle cups left over from their anniversary bash?"

"Does TV have girls with three names?" my bud responded. "Yes, girlfriend. There's a mountain of them gathering dust in our five-car garage. I mean, they would be gathering dust if our cleaning crew were less efficient. Why do you ask?"

There was this click on the line. "Summer, is that your call waiting or mine?" I asked.

"Yours," De said.

"Okay, I'll be right back. Hang on." I pressed call waiting. *"Bueno?"* I said.

"Hey, Cher, it's Brandon," the poet said cautiously. "Is it too late to call?"

"Too late as in past phone call curfew?" I said. "Or too late as in you left Ani's bungalow without so much as a goodbye?"

"I'm kind of lame on multiple choice, Cher. I do much better on essay tests." There was no smile in the boy's voice. He sounded sad, like seriously remorseful.

"Are you okay?" I asked.

"Sure," he said unconvincingly. Then after a brief pause, he went. "Actually, it's been a rough day."

"Tell me about it," I agreed. "Aside from my epic conversation with Ani, who is definitely all that, I could have taken a pass on the total twenty-four. Candidly, Brandon, your exit so did not make a bad day better."

"I'm calling to apologize," he said.

I jumped onto my bed and leaned back against the pile of plush pillows from Odalisque on Beverly Boulevard, where Madonna sightings are frequent. "Be my guest," I said.

"Okay, I'm sorry, Cher."

"Oh, that's poetic."

"Poetry starts with telling the truth," Brandon said. "And this is the truth. I am sorry. I wanted to stay. I wanted to be with you. I like being with you, Cher."

"But?" I prompted.

"But I saw you with that muscle-bound Moe, that costumed cadet wearing Michael Bolton's old hair."

I stifled a laugh. "You mean Troy?"

"Troy. Whatever," Brandon went on. "And when that bogus stooge picked you up like a slab of meat and bragged about what a big fan of his you were . . . I guess it was the last straw. The straw that cracked the old camel's back. The ripe cherry on my stress-flavored sundae."

"You mean," I said softly, "you were jealous?"

"I just didn't like the way that twenty-something toadhead was treating you." Brandon deftly evaded my question. "And it wasn't like I was having a great time before that."

"Por que?" I said Spanishly. "Why not?"

"Your friend Amber broke the news that she'd made a little mistake about her father's patient," Brandon said. "It isn't Harold Shomsky who's psychotic. It's that billionaire butcher from Bel Air."

"Henry Chumpkin, the mail-order steak king," I said. "I guess that's why his ads all say, 'Our prices are . . . craaaazy!' "

That earned a chuckle from the bummed-out boy. "So, anyway," he said, "I just called to apologize for ducking out that way."

"Well, I'm glad you did," I confessed. "I had this teeny-weeny icky thought that it might have been something I did or said. I mean, it was just this passing notion. I try not to offend. Usually, I'm excellent with people."

"You thought it was your fault?" Brandon asked.

"Not." I quickly straightened him out. "I told you, it was just like for a second." Suddenly, I was very tired. I yawned and stretched.

"It's late, isn't it?" Brandon said. "I'll let you go. Are we friends again?"

"Totally," I assured him. "See you tomorrow, okay?" I hung up, then clicked to see if De and Summer were still holding. They weren't. I closed my eyes and kind of dozed off with my shoes still on. Which I so hate. So, then I roused myself and rolled out of bed.

I was shuffling into the bathroom to brush my teeth, when I remembered the letter from Shomsky on Ani's wall. I glanced at my digital clock radio.

It was late, but like teenage late. Not adult Ani kind of late. Daddy wasn't even home yet. I was all, Should I? Shouldn't I? for like a minute. Then I dialed Ani's number.

Tom answered. He asked me to hold on. Which I did. Then, a minute later, Ani was going, "Cher? What's wrong? Are you all right?"

I told her I was fine and apologized for calling after ten. "Two things," I said. "One is that there was this guy at your house today who you never got to meet. He's like soooo nice. And way bright. And a fully accomplished poet for a high school boy. His name is Brandon."

"Is he your sweetheart?" the bestselling romance writer naturally asked.

"We may be moving in that direction," I candidly confided. "But the def boy suffered a heinous setback today." I explained what had happened.

"So he's the author of *The Tender Tempest?*" Ani asked. "I think that's one of the stories Devora picked as a contest finalist. I look forward to reading it."

Suddenly, I thought of Amber. And not with the desire to heave. I felt a rush of sympathy for the girl. De and I had known the fashion victim forever, like almost since she was just a tasteless toddler. Plus we knew her parents, Tripp and Ginger.

Tripp, the eminent physician and family money machine, was in constant contact with his inner wuss.

Amber and her mother pumped him for cash so constantly that he could have had ATM behind his name instead of M.D. While Ginger, from whom Amber got her dyed red hair, was the face you saw in the dictionary next to the word *pushy*. So our childhood colleague hadn't had it easy.

"Well, you could say he cowrote it," I hedged. "Anyway, Brandon would really like to meet your friend Harold Shomsky. He so admires the famous poet and wants to get into his summer workshop."

"I'll see what I can do," Ani promised. "I don't suppose your father is there right now—"

"He's not home yet. But I thought you didn't want to speak to him on the phone," I said.

"I don't, but I may have to. I promised you I'd work something out fast." She gave this little laugh. "Cher, I've been trying to figure out how to do this thing. I'd like to just bump into him casually, socially. I don't want to turn this into high drama. You'd think a novelist would know how to set up a romantic scene, wouldn't you? But I'm stuck."

"Awesome!" I exclaimed. "I mean, that's the other reason I called. Ani, I think I've got the perfect plan."

Chapter 14

Saturday turned out to be the most props day ever for a celebration of love.

From Summer's parents' weekend palazzo, high in the Santa Monica hills, you could see the vast Pacific. Tubular waves with little bitty surfers on their backs crashed against the beaches of Malibu, while sunshine peeked through the churning blades of celebrity-hunting helicopters overhead.

On Friday afternoon, De and I had realized that we'd need help setting up our gift. Lots of help. Like three boys' worth. So we had wangled last-minute invites for Murray, Sean, and Brandon. And Friday night, our trippin' team transported Ben's babies and boxes of De's heartshaped candle cups to Summer's house.

The same crew showed up on Saturday in chronic party togs.

Everyone, including Daddy, was duded up in their

jiggy best. Even Brandon wore a props blazer with his wrinkled chinos, white Pumas, and snug Calvin Klein charcoal-black T-shirt.

"I don't know why you need me now," Daddy said as we drove toward the bash. "You've got friends with you. If anything goes wrong, I'm sure the vet's grandson picked up a few Vietnam moves that'll come in handy."

"His name's Brandon, Daddy. And I don't need you with me for protection. I want you with me because I love you and I'm proud of you." It was true. I was kvelling at how fine Daddy looked in his double-breasted Hugo Boss suit, Venetian blue shirt, and red silk Sulka tie with pocket hanky to match.

"I love you, too, Pumpkin," he said as we pulled up in front of the Finkel-Dworkin mansion on the hill. "Or I'd never have given up my golf game today."

"I appreciate the sacrifice, Daddy," I said, after he handed his keys to the parking attendant. "And I promise you'll have an amazing time."

"Whatever happened to all those goldfish you were ladling out last night?" he asked.

"It's a surprise." I looked down the drive. De's car was only one BMW back. "You like surprises, don't you, Daddy?"

"As long as they're not in my soup," he joked. "Of course, I like surprises, Pumpkin." He patted my head affectionately, heinously smushing my shimmering 'do.

I ducked out from under his hand. "Then you're going to have a great time today," I promised as my best bud's Lexus pulled into the valet zone.

De and the boys hopped out. "Okay, now, at the ultimate moment, you're going to carry out the goldfish, right?" She was prepping our team.

"And the ultimate moment is?" Sean asked.

De groaned.

"It's right after the hors d'oeuvres and just before Ani Niel gives her speech," Brandon said.

"I knew that." Sean grinned. "I was just double-checking."

"I'm gonna double-check your brains," Murray warned.

De took Daddy's other arm, and the six of us headed inside.

"Ani Niel? Isn't she that author who reduced you to tears?" Daddy asked gruffly. "Why do people have to write books like that anyway? Isn't there enough to cry about in real life?"

"Daddy, she's a wonderful writer and a wonderful human being," I said. De coughed a warning.

But Daddy's legal mind snapped like a steel trap on my minor faux pas. "How do you know what kind of person she is?"

"Because she came to our school," De blurted out, trying to cover my error.

"Actually, I never met her," I said at the exact same time. "I just imagine her that way. You know, nice."

"And I imagined that she came to our school," De said quickly.

"That's it." Brandon snapped his fingers as though he'd just remembered the event. "It was in school. But we never met her because—"

"She wasn't really there," Sean jumped in. "I mean, not in person. She was on TV. In our school."

"Closed circuit," Murray improvised.

"Or maybe it was on the Internet. Yeah, that's it," Sean decided. "It was in this chat room on the Net."

Daddy turned to him sharply.

"Totally family programming, sir," Sean said quickly.

"Yet interactive," De added. "Which is why I mistakenly thought we'd actually met her."

Daddy was befuddled. But we were inside the house now, and there were so many people milling about and so much noise all at once that there was no way we could continue the conversation.

I spotted Summer through the crowd. She was miles away, standing at the sliding glass doors to the garden. The slinky red dress we'd snagged at Bloomie's looked even better on her than I remembered.

Grabbing De's hand, I hollered to Daddy, "Just mingle. We'll be back."

He waved and nodded, and we were Audi with the boy-bud trio hot on our spiky heels.

"Excuse me," Sean said as we moved through the mob. "Did I miss something? Is there anyone under baby-boomer age at this blowout?"

"Yeah," Murray said, "I haven't seen a crowd this wrinkled since the raptor stampede in *The Lost World*."

"Hey, Summer, wicked blowout." I hugged our glammed-up homey. "You look fabby in that frock."

Summer did this little twirl. "Don't you love it."

"Lose the seashell necklace and feather earrings," De advised.

"You guys look furiously flash, too," Summer squealed, obediently unfastening her necklace. "Cher, your goldfish idea is so clean! My folks are gonna freak totally."

"Well, I was thinking, you know, goldfish, Goldie Finkel-Dworkin, it just sounded right."

"And they're going to look so adorable swimming around in those heart-shaped little bowls," De said.

"Do you think there'll be enough for every table?" Summer asked.

De and I looked at each other. We'd scooped up over six hundred little goldfish last night. "Ben furiously outdid the McCaugheys," I assured Summers.

"Yeah, we're figuring about a dozen cups of baby goldfish per table," Murray said. "Er, Summer, nothing personal, but are all your parents' friends old?"

"Duh. Why do think I invited you guys?" she said. "Come on, there's a dance band down at the gazebo."

"Right between walker parking and the oxygen tanks," Sean muttered.

"I'm going to look for Ani," I said.

"I'll stay with you," Brandon offered. "If that's okay?"

"Doable," I decided.

Murray, De, and Sean took off with Summer. It was so jammed in the house that Brandon had to hold my hand so we wouldn't get separated.

We did a couple of laps without an author sighting. "I need air," I called, starting to feel hemmed in by overdressed adults marinated in Polo, Chanel, and Obsession.

"This way." Brandon tugged me toward the kitchen, which was almost as bustling as the party props. Catering cuties in black-and-white uniforms were loading up trays and taking off with military precision. "So this is where the Gen-Xers hang," Brandon noted. "Maybe we should send up a flare for Sean and Murray."

"Our buds will find them soon enough. They're carrying food," I pointed out.

We followed a boy with a tray full of bacon-wrapped chicken livers out into the service yard. "Eew," I went, lifting the hem of my ankle-length draped rayon jersey dress. My strappy sandals were not going to make it through the melting ice cubes and spilled food scraps.

Suddenly, Brandon swept me up into his arms. It was like the Troy episode, only without the body oil and pancake makeup rubbing off on my choice apparel. Plus the boy smelled so clean. He was an oasis of soap in a world of spritz.

Kicking open a wooden gate, he carried me over the gucky puddles and out into the garden.

A pebbled path ran through these amazing flower beds which were separated from the main grounds by towering hedges.

Here and there, little concrete benches were set in bowers of climbing yellow roses, pink bougainvillea, and white and pale-purple wisteria.

The mob hadn't found this floral fairyland yet. We could hear talking and laughing and glasses clinking on the other side of the hedge.

Brandon set me down gently on one of the benches. "Thanks," he said.

"For what?" I looked up at him. "I'm the grateful one, from the bottom of my Manolo Blahnik footwear, which would so not have survived that service yard."

"Thanks for setting up this thing with Shomsky. I can't believe I'm going to meet him tonight," he said, looking down at me.

"Ani put it all in motion," I said. Harold Shomsky was giving a poetry reading in Westwood. Ani had reserved seats for us there. And she'd promised to introduce Brandon to the poet.

Standing above me, Brandon took my face in his hands, just as he had at the beach. He lowered his head until his lips were inches from mine. "Yeah, but if it hadn't been for you, Cher . . ." he started to say.

"Sssshh," I went suddenly.

"What is it?" Brandon whispered.

"Your worst nightmare," I whispered back. "I think I heard Daddy's voice behind the hedge."

The babe straightened up abruptly. "You're kidding, right?"

I wasn't. "And he's wearing his Hugo Boss suit and Gucci loafers," I said. "Full uniform."

Brandon jumped back.

"Seriously, ssshh," I went. I got to my knees on the bench and tried to look through the bushes. It was no use. All I could see through the dense shrubbery were dark shapes moving slightly.

"Well, you're nothing like I expected," Daddy was saying.

"Really?"

It was Ani! I could hear her tinkly laugh.

I stood up on the bench. Even in my highest heels, I couldn't see over the top of the hedge.

"I don't know," Daddy said. "When I walked into my daughter's room and saw her crying, crying over a story, a book, *your* book . . ." There was this pause. I could just imagine him shaking his head. "Well, I guess I jumped to conclusions."

"Contempt before investigation, counselor?" Ani said. Again, there was that lightness in her voice, that little silver laugh. "You seem like such a sensible man."

"Silly, huh?" Daddy said. "But Cher's just so special to me. I can't stand to see her unhappy. I mean I know now, because you explained it, that she was just relating to the book. That she'd fallen in love with the characters and hated to lose them. I never really thought of it that way."

I was stretched so high on my tiptoes that I started swaying. I almost fell into the hedge. I waved my arms around trying to get my balance.

Suddenly, Brandon caught my waist to steady me. His touch startled me and I yelped.

"What was that?" Daddy asked.

We froze.

"It sounds like someone's behind the hedge," Ani said. "The kitchen's back there. The service area, I think."

"Well, anyway," Daddy continued after a moment. "I obviously overreacted. I thought you were to blame. Of course, that was before I met you."

"My father was overprotective, too," Ani said, softly. "Parents often misinterpret things."

"Pick me up," I whispered to Brandon, motioning for him to hoist me onto his shoulders. He looked at me like I'd gone mental. Then he smiled, shrugged, and lifted me up.

It was an awkward move. We tried to be really quiet about it.

"He was probably just looking out for your best interests," Daddy was saying to Ani. "Are you sure we've never met? You just seem so familiar to me."

I craned my neck. My nose barely grazed the bushes. I leaned down trying not to topple us over. "Brandon," I whispered, "can you get up on the bench?"

"With you on my shoulders?" he said, brown eyes buggin'.

I nodded.

"So where did you say you're from?" Daddy asked Ani. "Holmby Hills?"

"That's where I live now," she answered. "I moved there just a few months ago."

I was swaying on Brandon's shoulder as he attempted to climb onto the bench. I gripped his hair to balance myself.

"Yeow," he cried softly.

"That must be why I've never run into you," Daddy said. "Where are you from originally?"

Brandon had made it. I was head and shoulders above the top of the hedge. Out in front of me was this enormous lawn with a giant tent set up smack in the middle of it. The tent was surrounded by row upon row of round dining tables covered with pink linen cloths and garlanded in roses.

And there were people everywhere! I could see hundreds of them. But I couldn't see Daddy and Ani, who were directly below us. So, still grasping Brandon's head, I leaned forward carefully.

"Originally, I'm from Brooklyn," Ani was saying.

"No kidding. You won't believe this," Daddy said. "I'm from Brooklyn, too."

I could see them now! They were standing, facing each other. Ani was looking right at Daddy. "I know, Melvin," she said.

"Melvin?" Daddy laughed. "Gee, it's been a long time since anyone—" Suddenly, he took hold of her shoulders. "Holy cow!" Daddy said. "It's you!"

Ani was nodding.

"It's you, Ina, isn't it?" Daddy shouted.

I was leaning too far forward. Brandon started rocking.

From behind us, Summer's voice rang out. "I found them! Cher, it's goldfish time, girlfriend!"

I shrieked and tumbled forward. Brandon tried to hang on to me and went crashing through the bushes. De and Murray and Sean started screaming.

I got one quick glimpse of Daddy's face before I fell from the sky and bowled him over. He was way surprised.

Ani shrieked and jumped back. And then she started laughing. She had the best laugh ever. It was like music, like medicine.

My buds came scrambling through the smashed hedge to help us up. And then the orchestra in the gazebo started playing the "Wedding March." Ani went, "Yikes, that's my cue. Are you okay, Melvin?"

Daddy looked up from the ground and nodded. Then he looked at me. I was kind of sprawled out, leaning back on my elbows. "Whoops?" I said, all blue-eyed and innocent.

"Whoops?" Daddy said. "That's it? Is that all you've got to say for yourself?" He shook his head, then he reached over and messed up my hair. And then he started to laugh.

We all did.

Brandon, whose khakis were torn at the knee, reached down. I thought he was going to pull me up. But it was Daddy he extended his hand to.

Daddy glanced at me. "You okay, Pumpkin?" he asked.

"Stellar," I assured him. He took Brandon's hand, and the buff poet hauled him to his feet.

"Thanks," Daddy said, brushing off his pinstriped Boss and adjusting his pocket hanky.

Brandon shrugged modestly. Then, right in front of Daddy, Ani, and everyone, he reached down and scooped me up into his arms again.

There I was, arms wrapped around the props poet's neck, strappy spike-heeled sandals dangling five feet off the ground, my jersey-draped self snug against Brandon's ripply muscled, Calvin-clad chest.

Daddy cleared his throat meaningfully.

But Ani beamed at us. She took Daddy's hand.

"Melvin, we've got so much to catch up on," she said, leading him away.

I could feel Brandon's soapy sweet face against my cheek.

"Look at you," De said, grinning. "You look like the cover of a romance novel."

"Word up," Murray agreed. "It's a total smooch scene, an epic bonding tableau."

"White Pumas and torn chinos beat buckskin tights any day," Sean insisted.

"You guys!" Summer was wiggin'. "It's time!"

And as Brandon's lips at long last meshed with mine, all my buds hurried off to carry heart-shaped bowls of little bitty goldfish to each table . . . with our love.

About the Author

H. B. Gilmour is the author of the best-selling novelizations *Clueless* and *Pretty in Pink* as well as *Clueless™: Cher's Guide to . . . Whatever;* the Clueless novels *Achieving Personal Perfection, Friend or Faux, Baldwin from Another Planet, Cher and Cher Alike, Romantically Correct, A Totally Cher Affair,* and *Babes in Boyland; Clarissa Explains It All: Boys;* the well-reviewed young-adult novel *Ask Me If I Care;* and more than fifteen other books for adults and young people.